Cocaineros Duel

by

John J. Gilmore

Mainly Murder Press, LLC

PO Box 290586
Wethersfield, CT 06109-0586
www.mainlymurderpress.com

Mainly Murder Press

Copy Editor: Jack Ryan
Executive Editor: Judith K. Ivie
Cover Designer: Karen Phillips

Mainly Murder Press
www.mainlymurderpress.com

Copyright © 2010 by John J. Gilmore
ISBN 978-0-9827952-1-7

Published in the United States of America

Mainly Murder Press
PO Box 290586
Wethersfield, CT 06109-0586

For Mary

… my wife, my best friend and my editor. Through the days and nights of writing, rewriting and editing, she was there, giving me the best counsel. It was her "final eyes" that found the errors of grammar and logic that sneak into every manuscript in the dark of night.

One

Captain Guillermo Garcia Ruiz arrived at the hotel room and eyed a police officer getting ready to close the zipper on the body bag. The captain motioned with his finger for a team of cops to stop what they were doing while he bent over to stare at the swollen and beaten face of a woman. She had been dead for several hours. Both her eyes were black and blue, and there was a cut starting at the end of her left eye that traveled up to the middle of her forehead. There were several cuts in the soft flesh of her cheeks. One ear had a severe gash. Ruiz was appalled at the rage the killer must have had to kill a woman so violently with his bare hands.

The captain continued to stare at the body while one of the cops explained that the preliminary assessment from the doctor was the woman died from blows delivered by her assailant's hands and not a weapon. Ruiz eyed the cop. He was angered by the understatement of the cop giving his report. While Ruiz fought to keep his emotions in check, the policeman was spouting out raw facts without any concern the body before him was once a living human being.

"We have not found any blunt instruments with blood that match the wounds," the cop said, anticipating his captain's question. The cop continued to repeat the doctor's assessment that the woman suffered multiple fractures and that any single one of several blows could have caused her death. The captain nodded without looking at his subordinate.

"Where is the doctor?" Ruiz asked.

"He left. He said his work was finished," the cop said.

"Not yet," the captain said, angered by the man's departure before his arrival. "Have him report to my office immediately and wait for me, and instruct him to bring everything he has pertaining to the case," Ruiz said. "And I mean everything."

"Yes, sir," the cop said, pulling out a cell phone to make the call and thankful he wasn't going to be on the receiving end of Ruiz's wrath.

Ruiz straightened himself up and scanned the room. He said nothing as he assessed the mess about him. Ruiz was always appalled by murders. The murder of an American in his jurisdiction was sure to bring complications. Drawers were ripped out of the cheap wooden bureau in the corner. Clothes were emptied out of the suitcases and tossed all over the room. Hangers were stripped off the pole in the closet. The shower curtain was torn from its rail and abandoned on the floor. The mattress had been pulled off the bed frame and sliced open with a knife. The corners of the wall-to-wall carpeting were also pulled up.

The killers wanted something, Ruiz thought to himself. This wasn't a simple robbery. If it were a robbery, they simply would have killed her and taken what they wanted. No, these killers beat this woman for information and for something she hid from them. He wondered if the killers found the prize they were looking for in this hotel room.

Ruiz stared down at the dead woman. The veteran police captain understood there was violence in the world and in his country. He just couldn't bring himself to accept it. He walked around the hotel room, continuing to take in the scene.

The cop kneeling by the body bag hadn't stirred. He was waiting for another order from Ruiz, but the captain stood silent.

Another cop approached the captain with the woman's purse. "We found this," he said, handing Ruiz a faded photograph. The cop also held a handful of identification papers that he had found tossed about the room.

First, the captain inspected the old picture intently. He stared at the image of a young man at a beach with a woman. He looked back at the dead woman, studying her beaten and swollen face. Through the injuries on her face, Ruiz saw similarities. He inspected the identification documents. His eyes shifted back to the photograph, specifically the image of the young man. The nature of the clues started to come together in his mind.

Finally, with an air of confidence, he said, "Get me the *Yanqui* called Reardon. He has a fishing boat at the docks."

The cop who brought the purse nodded.

Ruiz signaled for the other cop to zip up the body bag and continue the crime scene procedures with his team.

"Bring Reardon to my office," Ruiz commanded.

Frank Reardon came out of the fish shack carrying an ice-cold *Presidente* beer and a hot Cuban sandwich. It was a perfect day to do nothing. He strolled down the pier to the dock where his fishing boat was tied up. The sun beat down and warmed the pier. The blue Caribbean lapped the shoreline, and in the distance he saw the top of his boat. He had arrived in Central America three months ago, and life was good. He picked up some cash once in a while by taking cruise ship tourists in Limon on fishing trips along the Costa Rican coast. With the help of some secondhand tour books, he could easily talk his way through an afternoon of fishing. When times were slow, he drifted up and down the coast exploring small fishing villages and the coves and inlets they offered.

Life in the Caribbean was carefree for Frank. He settled into a day-to-day existence easily. He didn't care what day it was and had less and less interest in the world he left behind. Sometime after leaving the United States, he even abandoned wearing a wristwatch. It was useless in his new life. He ate when he was hungry and slept when he was tired. The new lifestyle agreed with him. More than middle-aged but not quite a senior citizen, Frank still had life left in him. He planned to make the most of it.

As Frank strolled closer to his boat, the *Celtic Mistress*, he spotted a police jeep on the road above the boatyard. A cop in a khaki uniform sat in the passenger seat. Smoke from his cigarette streamed out of the canvas-topped vehicle parked in the shade under a coconut palm tree. He knew the drill. This cop, watching him approach in the jeep's oversized side view mirror, had him under surveillance. All sorts of instincts, the kind he had hoped were left behind in the States, were starting to kick in, and he wasn't enjoying the message he was reading.

Frank eyed the cop as he slowly stepped out of the four-wheel drive vehicle. Standing ramrod straight with his hands clasped behind his back, the cop wore a crisp, long-sleeved khaki shirt with sergeant chevrons on the sleeves, a thin black tie and matching khaki slacks. The brim of his military style eight-point service cap was pulled down to the top of the frame of his aviator sunglasses and hid any sign of emotion.

Slowly, Frank turned down onto the pier and saw two more cops by the gangplank of his boat. The underlings wore similar shirts with open collars, but no stripes, and matching short pants.

"This can't be good," Frank muttered to himself. "Not good at all."

The cops on the pier waved their arms furiously at Frank's dog, Dutch, who was barking and growling at them as they tried to inch across a gangplank and onto the deck of his boat. The German shepherd, showing his razor-sharp teeth, refused to surrender one inch of the *Celtic Mistress*'s deck to the cops.

"Dutch, quiet. Quiet down, Dutch!" Frank hollered as he ran toward the boat. Whatever these guys wanted didn't matter. Dutch was ready to tear off an arm or a leg.

The cops stopped trying to board the *Celtic Mistress* when they heard Frank holler at the dog. They turned and continued their screaming in Spanish at him.

"No hable Espanol," Frank yelled back. *"No hable Espanol. Ingles, por favor. Ingles."*

It was no use. As Frank sputtered in broken Spanish, the two cops kept hollering at him and pointing at the boat and Dutch. One of them waved papers clutched in his hand.

Suddenly, from behind, a voice yelled *"Silencio!"* It was the sergeant from the police car parked on the road above.

The sergeant barked orders in Spanish and took the papers from his underling.

"They felt threatened by your dog, *senor*. He upset them. They were sent to deliver these impound papers for your ..."

"Impound papers!" Frank yelled. "What do you mean?"

The cop sighed and said, "For your boat and to find you."

Frank backed off. It was time to let things play out. This was their country.

"Can we start over?" Frank sighed.

"Good," the sergeant said. "Your boat has been impounded to guarantee your cooperation in a police matter. Luckily, your dog never left the deck." Without the slightest hint of any possible remorse, he added, "Otherwise, my men might have been forced to shoot him."

Frank counted to three in his mind before speaking. "Yes," he said slowly, "luckily I came along. What needs my cooperation, sergeant?"

"If you'll come with me to headquarters, my captain will speak with you," he said calmly from behind his sunglasses.

"I'm happy to cooperate. Thank you for your restraint regarding Dutch. Can I stop at the fish shack and call a buddy to feed my dog?" Frank asked with a smile. "He'll only take food from certain people, and I've been gone all morning. He's hungry."

The sergeant thought for a moment. Then he nodded and said, "Make the call." After Frank made his call at the makeshift grocery store on the dock, they all piled into the police vehicle. The car sped along the coastal road from the fishing village to headquarters in Limon. No one spoke.

At police headquarters Frank was brought to a squad room and told to sit on a bench. *So far, so good,* Frank thought. *At least I'm not under arrest.*

For Frank, Costa Rica was a place to start over, to look at life from a different angle. After he retired from the Police Department in Bridgeport, Connecticut and after his wife Susan died, Frank had nothing. He didn't relish hanging around cop bars and telling war stories to rookies, so he quickly decided to leave his hometown and head south.

Dutch was a last-minute addition to his life. The German shepherd was a true junkyard dog. He became Frank's just before he was to be put down.

After a half-hour of waiting on the wooden bench, Frank was ushered in to Captain Ruiz.

"*Senor*, thank you for coming in," Captain Ruiz said from behind a large oak desk. It reminded Frank of furniture used by titans of industry in late night movies.

"My pleasure," Frank answered. *As if there was a choice implied,* he thought. The impound papers for the *Celtic Mistress* probably bore this cop's signature.

"You are *Senor* Frank Reardon?" he asked while looking over a file in front of him.

"Yes," Frank said.

"You own the boat known as *Celtic Mistress* in our docks?" he asked. Frank noticed he pronounced it *sell-teck.* He thought it better not to correct him.

"I do, and it is," Frank said calmly.

"I understand you are a police officer in *Norte America*?" Ruiz continued.

"I used to be. I'm retired now." *This cop had me checked out,* Frank thought.

"How long have you been in Costa Rica, *Senor* Reardon?" he asked.

"I've been up and down the coast of Central America from Mexico to Panama for the past three months, captain. I've been in and out of Costa Rica several times. Is there something specific you want to know?" Frank probed.

"I see," the captain said with a deliberate pause. Captain Ruiz was slowly formulating in his mind a series of questions. He was in no hurry.

Ruiz stood up and walked to the window. He stared out for a moment at the palm tree-lined boulevard below his office. In the distance he could see the tall, stately Ceiba trees in a local park. The trees were considered sacred by the indigenous people of the country.

The police captain, too, wore the same smartly pressed khaki shirt and pants as the sergeant, but his shirt bore epaulettes with the twin gold bars denoting a captain's rank. *Railroad tracks*, Frank thought to himself, remembering the military slang for the bars. *Let's hope those railroad tracks don't indicate something to come.*

Captain Ruiz stared out the window while Frank surveyed the cop's office. The walls were peppered with a collection of photographs of the captain shaking hands with an array of men in suits. They were all Hispanic, dark skinned, mustachioed, a few with beards, and some wearing medals. All looked powerful and prosperous. One face jumped off the wall. It was the only face he recognized. The picture showed Ruiz standing before a podium at a large dinner gathering with Cuban strongman Fidel Castro in his heyday. *He's a social butterfly*, Frank thought to himself, *a political wannabe*.

Frank figured the other men in the photos had to be political big shots from around Central America. He'd seen this type of picture collection at home. All over the United States, small-time politicians collected and displayed photographs of themselves shaking hands with congressmen, senators, judges, any bigwig they could find, all to imply that they, by association, had juice. It was classic blue smoke and mirrors: Get power by making someone believe you already had it.

"I must tell you, *senor*, I have been trained at your Federal Bureau of Investigation Training Academy at Quantico, Virginia, in *los Estados Unidos*," he declared with pride. "You know this school?" he asked.

"Yes, captain, I do. Many police officers in the United States go there for advanced training. I, too, went there." Frank felt obligated to play his game and throw him a bone.

"Truly? *Bueno*! We are then, how do you say, fellow alumni." Captain Ruiz beamed.

"Well, yes, I guess we are," Frank laughed.

Both men were twirling around the floor in a police dance choreographed with questions and answers. Frank knew, as did the captain, who was leading the dance. The cop called the tune, and all Frank could hope for was that the music didn't stop and leave him in an ugly place.

"Yes," the captain continued, "I was sent to *los Estados Unidos* as part of your country's efforts to train policemen around the world in ways to combat drug trafficking. I plan to go back again as part of your country's fight against terrorists, too. So much to learn," the captain said.

Frank needed to make the captain lay his cards on the table. "Captain, you have something on your mind. If I can help, please tell me," he declared.

"Ah, to the point, I appreciate that, *senor*. Although, I thought we were enjoying our conversation?" Captain Ruiz queried. "No matter, we will do it your way," he said. "Here, let me show you a *fotografia*. It's a *fotografia* of you, I believe. I say this because my last trip to Quantico was for a course on how to identify people in the present from *fotografias* of the past. Not a perfect science, of course, but an investigative technique gaining use in light of the growing terrorism issue. Is this not you, *senor*?"

With the flair of a Las Vegas magician, the captain produced an aging snapshot of a young man and a girl on a beach hugging each other in a pose for the camera. Frank looked at the picture and recognized it immediately. It was a snapshot of Frank and Cheryl Norris, a girl he dated in college, taken long before his marriage to Susan. The picture was of the couple at Hammonasset State Park, a beach in Connecticut. For a second Frank was transported to New England until a Spanish accent yanked him back to Costa Rica.

"*Senor*? I ask you again, is this not you?" the cop asked. "I traced the license plate on the car shown here. This was your car," Ruiz charged. "This is you," he said, tapping the picture. There was no more cop-to-cop banter. The tone was now cop-to-perp.

Frank was dumbstruck. Where the hell did he get this photograph? It was of him and Cheryl in an old car he owned years ago. What was this wrinkled, fading picture doing in Central America? He looked at the captain and mentally collected himself.

"Yes, it's me, what of it?" Frank asked calmly. "Where did you get it?"

"I will be asking all the questions, *senor*! Do you understand?" Dropping his palms on the top of the oversized desk, the captain asked, "And the woman, who is she?" He paused for effect between each word. "What is her name?"

"Her name is Cheryl, Cheryl Norris, but you probably know that fact," Frank said. "What you really want to know is my relationship with her. She's an old girlfriend, one from a very long time ago," he said. "The picture shows that."

Frank wanted to start leading his own dance now. The picture showed a relationship, nothing else. Frank had to keep talking but say nothing. If he could do it fast enough, maybe, just maybe, this cop would let some new information drop. He needed to discover how good Ruiz had been in interrogation class at Quantico.

"Yes, it very clearly shows that," Captain Ruiz said. "When did you see her last?"

"I don't know, maybe twenty years ago. Maybe more, why?" Frank asked.

"Don't lie to me. When did you see her last?" the captain repeated.

"Captain, you're headed somewhere. Why don't you just lay it all out? I'm in the dark here, and I fear this situation and our bantering is just aggravating you unnecessarily," Frank said.

"Very well," Captain Ruiz said, "as a former police officer I'm sure you will understand my point of view and display of temper."

Frank nodded, curious to hear more.

"I have a body, *senor*. In fact I have the body of a dead woman in the morgue, an American woman. And the slim materials of identification I have about this woman link her to you, an American with, well, with less than stable roots in my country. Further, her death was not pleasant or accidental."

Frank froze. He was speechless. He knew nothing about Cheryl's death or, for that matter, about her life since he last saw her. Then, without realizing it, his brain shifted into cop-mode.

"Materials of identification?" he asked. "What materials? And I want to see the body. How did she die, exactly, how did she die? And where and when, captain? I'll need all these answers if I'm going to help. You did secure the crime scene?"

The Limon cop was instantly confused. A few moments ago he believed he had a suspect sitting in his office. Now he was hearing a seasoned investigator, and the questions kept coming.

Frank stood and walked in a circle, holding the photograph and tapping it against the fingers of his other hand. "Captain, I assume you had this picture dusted for fingerprints before you and I started thumbing it today? You really should have left it in an evidence bag," Frank rattled on. He was fully engaged in a frame of mind from a past that he desperately wanted to abandon. But that old "cop" state of mind was protecting him now.

"And your immigration service, I assume you checked as to when she crossed into Costa Rica. Was she alone? We'll need to know," Frank said.

Frank was on a roll. He kept firing questions faster and faster. "Her personal effects?" he queried. "Luggage, jewelry, we should look at everything."

The captain stood there in total confusion. He had lost control of the interview and now wasn't sure if he had a new partner or a supervising detective.

"Captain? Captain? Did you hear me? I'll need to see your file on this case after I see the body," Frank said.

"Stop!" the cop screamed. "*Silencio!*"

Frank stood still and shot an innocent look at the captain. Had he pressed his game too far? "I'm sorry, Captain Ruiz. You wanted to say something," Frank offered.

Captain Ruiz was starting to seethe. "Yes, *senor*. Before we continue, please tell me," the captain said, forcing calm into each word, "where were you all day yesterday and last night?"

"Me, captain? Where was I? Oh, yes, you need to cover the bases. I see, well, I was alone aboard the *Celtic Mistress*. Just me and Dutch, my dog," Frank said. He didn't have a better alibi, just the truth, and thought that might not be enough. This captain just might be able to hang a killing on him. Before that happened, Frank wanted to muddy things for this Costa Rican social climber. Frank wished he had a better story, but for now the truth was the truth. Another truth was Ruiz didn't have much evidence anyway. Unfortunately for Frank, this was Ruiz's turf.

"Captain, let's be honest. Alone? On a boat with a dog? Not much of an alibi, we both know that. But really," Frank bluffed, "unless you have more than a snapshot, I don't need one, do I? So where do we go from here?" he asked.

It was time for the captain to make a move, any move. Frank's ability to wrest control of the interview upset Ruiz and gave him a headache. The captain chose to stall his final move. He needed time to assess things.

Ruiz screamed for the sergeant outside. Before the sound of the command dissipated, the sergeant appeared in the office.

"Take *Senor* Reardon to see the victim's body. Then return here with him immediately. Do you understand?" the captain demanded.

"*Si, capitan*," the cop said.

Turning to Frank, the captain said, "For the moment you'll remain my guest, and then we'll see where we will go, *senor*. Do you understand? If you challenge me, we'll see how much authority I have and how much you have. You will cooperate, yes?"

"Yes, I will cooperate," Frank said. It was a good move by Ruiz. The cop had bought himself some time, and Frank knew he wouldn't waste it. Frank still needed to know who killed Cheryl and why it happened in Costa Rica at the same time he was in the country. The *fotografia* held by the captain was the only lead.

The sergeant and his two officers took Frank to the morgue in a hospital a few blocks from police headquarters. A doctor described the dead woman in the morgue as having been beaten beyond recognition by someone very powerful. The doctor said the assailant appeared to have committed the assault with bare hands, not a weapon.

"Are you sure?" Frank asked.

"Central America and parts of South America provide our world of medicine with a great many opportunities to see man's inhumanity," the doctor said. "People in this part of the world suffer greatly at the hands of the drug traffickers, rebels, various armies and a host of experts in thievery. Cases are very different here than those among the rich people in *los Estados Unidos*," he lectured.

"Trust me, doctor," Frank answered, "emergency rooms in my country see things just as inhuman."

The morgue technician popped the cooler door open and pulled out the tray. He grabbed the sheet that covered a female body and flipped it off her face down to her neck. The cops turned away in horror. The tech straightened the pens in his shirt pocket.

Frank said nothing. He noted the reaction of the cops as he assessed the body before him. The woman's face was beaten black and blue and was still grotesquely swollen. There were rough cuts on the edges of her face by her eyes and around the corners of her forehead. Frank had seen boxers suffer these edge cuts but never so many at one time.

"Cover her up," he commanded.

The technician flipped the sheet back over the dead woman's head and started to slide the tray back into the cooler. "No. Stop," Frank said. He reached under the sheet and slowly took the dead woman's right hand in his and removed it from underneath its covering. Tenderly, he stroked the back of her hand and stared at the covered body. He spread the fingers apart and gently rubbed each one individually. He pressed them together again and went back to caressing the back of her hand. With care, he patted the hand and placed it back under the sheet.

"Take me back to the captain," he ordered. "Now."

The cops stared at each other. Who was in charge, they wondered? Frank didn't wait for them to process the scene in the morgue. He was out the door and heading down the hall to the police car in the driveway. At the police car, Frank jumped into the front passenger seat and stared straight ahead.

"I'll sit up front this time, if you don't mind. Let's go, your captain is waiting." The sergeant stared at Frank and saw the coldest pair of eyes he had ever seen. Then Frank turned his head away. Subconsciously, the sergeant knew he had just experienced a very dangerous man.

The trip to the morgue gave Frank all the leverage he'd need over Captain Ruiz.

Two

Frank and his police escorts arrived back at headquarters, and he was immediately brought to Ruiz's office. The captain was staring out the window, hands clasped behind him in the familiar military at-ease position.

"So, *Senor* Reardon, now that you have seen the woman's body and the savageness of the crime, you understand why I am, how do you say, terse with you. Such brutal acts demand swift police action," the captain said. "I believe you are involved, and I want some answers now," the captain demanded.

Frank didn't respond, and Ruiz never turned around to look at him. The silence continued. Finally, the captain turned around to find Frank smiling and looking for a chair.

Frank slid into a chair next to the desk. He crossed his legs and got comfortable. Looking up at Ruiz he declared, "You have a big problem, *amigo*."

"Problem, *senor*?" the captain asked. "Explain," he demanded.

"Your victim is not Cheryl Norris. I don't know who she is, captain. But she is without a doubt not Cheryl Norris," Frank said.

He stared at the captain's crisp khaki uniform and was impressed that it still held its sharp creases in the muggy Costa Rican weather. Frank's own appearance was less impressive. He was dressed in faded hiking shorts and a commemorative T-shirt from a charity bicycle ride several years earlier in Vermont. Also, he needed a shave. Nevertheless, Frank was now in charge.

"What do you mean? I have her papers, her passport, the *fotografia* of you and her together. You admitted knowing her!" the cop sputtered. He withdrew a manila envelope from the drawer and held it upside down. The passport and other papers fell from the envelope and scattered across the desktop. "Why do you say this woman is not the American Cheryl Norris identified here?" the captain continued. It was the moment Frank had been waiting for, the moment the captain showed all his cards.

Leaning over the mess of papers, Frank slowly lifted out the passport and opened it. It bore Cheryl's name, but the picture on the document was of someone else. The woman bore a resemblance to Cheryl and could be easily mistaken for her by someone who didn't know either one very well. Frank knew instantly it was the victim. Ruiz had gotten that much right.

"Captain, Cheryl Norris, a woman we both agree I know, has a scar on the back of her right hand. It's a small, two-inch long, white-line scar. In fact, she was hurt in a bicycle accident that happened on the same day this picture was taken," he said, flipping the snapshot across the desk at the captain. "Your victim has no scar," Frank said.

"This Cheryl Norris, she is reported missing in *los Estados Unidos*, I checked," the captain countered.

"Maybe so," Frank said, "but you have no evidence she's dead in Costa Rica, and here, *mi amigo*, is where you have jurisdiction over crimes. Your victim is someone else. You have no evidence that I know this victim."

"I am going to hold you in custody until I clear up some issues, *senor*. I have a murder to solve and I believe you are involved," Captain Ruiz bellowed.

"I don't think so, *capitan*." Frank said. "You have no grounds to hold me and no evidence against me. I think I'll be going," Frank said as he stood up.

Despite his disheveled appearance, Frank still displayed a commanding presence. He retained a decent physique in retirement, the result of long walks and swimming. His hair was greying a bit, but it was still thick and wavy. With a shave and a change of clothes, he could make as impressive an appearance as Ruiz.

"Sit down, *senor*. Sit down now!" the captain said. "I will decide when and if you leave here. Only I will decide. You are in my custody, and in my custody you will stay."

Frank chuckled.

The laughter angered the police captain.

"*Telefono, capitan*," a clerk said, interrupting the interview.

"Get out!" he screamed at the clerk.

Frank sat smiling and shaking his head.

"You find this amusing?" the cop shot back.

"*Capitan*, my guess is that call you just ignored was from the American embassy," Frank said. "You can either call them back and get your orders or wait for them to come here from San Jose. I'll bet that forcing someone to make the trip from San Jose to Limon won't endear you to them. If that was the embassy, *capitan*, it was an official inquiry, and you appear to be short on answers. That means I can't get lost in your little bureaucratic network," Frank said.

Frank scanned the pictures on the wall, wondering if there was one showing the captain with the American ambassador.

"How did they know you were here?" Ruiz asked. "You made no calls."

"Well, that's not true," Frank explained. "Those guys you sent to pick me up, remember them? They let me make a call. I told them I needed someone to feed my dog, but I really called a buddy at the State Department and told him to have the embassy call here if I didn't call back in two hours."

"They let you make a telephone call?" Ruiz sputtered. "*Idiotas!*"

"*Capitan*, listen to me, you can still turn this around and not be embarrassed in front of the embassy. See the T-shirt Cheryl is wearing in this picture?" Frank asked, tapping the photograph.

The captain looked at him suspiciously.

"The lettering on the shirt is the name of the hospital where she was a nurse, the same hospital where she was treated after the bicycle accident. All you have to do is quietly ask someone at the State Department to unofficially ask for her medical records at the hospital to be pulled and inspected. The nature of her injury described by the doctor will confirm she probably ended up with a scar. And a scar on Cheryl proves you have a Jane Doe victim here in Limon. As for me, tell the State Department I'm just here to verify what you suspect to be the case. You simply recognized me from the picture and called me in," Frank offered. "It's neat, clean, and will hold up," Frank added.

The police captain was suspicious, but he didn't want to ignore the telephone call from the Americans or appear stupid before them. "Stay put," the captain ordered as he left the room.

After a while Captain Ruiz returned. "Get out, but remember me. I'll be watching you." He offered nothing about what he had learned about Cheryl.

Frank ambled slowly back to the docks. Before he had left the police station, the cops had returned his now cold Cuban sandwich and warm *Presidente* beer, but his mind was no longer on lunch.

Who is the woman in the morgue? How does Cheryl fit in? Or does she fit in? Frank knew there were too many questions and not enough answers. If Cheryl was in trouble somewhere in Costa Rica, he needed to find her and help her.

About a half a block down *Calle de San Ignacio,* Frank spotted a man in a blue and white seersucker suit crossing the street on an intercept path with him. He pegged him as an embassy guy. The man wore shiny black wing tips, a white button-down shirt and a small print tie. The stranger could have passed for a character from a Graham Greene novel or a model from a Brooks Brothers catalogue.

"Mr. Reardon, Mr. Reardon, please, I need a second of your time," he called.

Frank ducked and dodged through the crowd in the *mercado* off to the side of the plaza. The seersucker suit followed, his long American arm extended and finger wagging over the heads of shoppers. His calling went on nonstop.

Frank slowed his pace and allowed the embassy guy to close the gap. Finally, he stopped and spun around. The State Department official, still following under full steam, bumped into Frank.

"What?" Frank asked, grabbing the embassy man's arms and holding him in place.

"I need to speak with you," he huffed breathlessly. "I'm from the embassy."

"No kidding," Frank said. "Speak," he ordered.

"Here?" the embassy man asked.

"What's the matter? You don't like these people? It's their country, be polite!" Frank shot back. "You and I are the guests around here, or didn't they teach you that at diplomacy school?"

Grabbing his elbow and pushing him toward a sidewalk café, Frank commanded the man to sit. "*Dos cervesas, por favor,*" he said to a waiter.

"What's your name?" Frank asked.

"My name is Derrick Hines. I am a special advisor on the U.S. Embassy's Americans Living Abroad Team. We received a notice from the State Department that you contacted them directly about your arrest."

"I wasn't arrested," Frank interrupted.

"The police had you in custody. State said they arrested you. We could have helped you a lot faster," Derrick babbled on in the cafe.

Frank took a long sip on his beer and stared at Hines as he droned on.

"Who exactly did you call at State?" Derrick finally asked.

"Never mind," Frank replied. He knew what Derrick and the embassy in San Jose wanted. They wanted the name of Frank's source, his Washington contact. And that they couldn't have, ever.

"But Mr. Reardon, State called the embassy directly," Derrick continued. "If you tell me who you spoke with, I can report back that you've been released and ..."

"I'll make my own thank you's to my friend. You just report back through normal channels that I am out. Now, what else do you want?"

Derrick has the look of a blue blood, the son of old money, Frank thought. His demeanor hinted at a privileged upbringing. It was a good bet his daddy made regular and hefty campaign contributions to some politician in Washington. That made him someone within the State Department family who would be groomed and possibly fast-tracked for a better posting.

It was also a safe bet that Captain Ruiz knew Derrick's daddy and daddy's Washington friend, too. The cop was no fool. Networking was Ruiz's style.

No matter, Derrick served Frank's purpose. All Derrick had to do was follow orders. He had proved he could do that exceptionally well when he called Ruiz's office and advised him the State Department in Washington, not just the embassy, had an open eye regarding Frank's situation.

"Look, Derrick, you gonna drink that beer?" Frank didn't wait for a response. He just grabbed the bottle and took a swig.

"Well, as I started to say, Washington called and told us you were in custody. We were instructed to ask why and try and get you released. It was all very unusual for

Washington to call. If you will just tell me who you called?" he asked again.

"Never mind, what did they say?" Frank asked.

"They were unclear, and we had to make all sorts of inquiries and …"

"Not Washington, the cops, what did the cops say?" Frank asked.

"Oh, they said you were being questioned in connection with a murder, some American woman, rather unseemly type, I'm afraid," Derrick said.

"What else?" Frank pressed.

"Well," Derrick continued, "after a short while it became clear they were as confused as we were," he said.

"Who did you speak with?" Frank asked.

"At first, the sergeant, he gave me all the details and then I spoke with Capitan Guillermo Garcia Ruiz. He was very upset about the mystery over the identity of the victim. He felt the sergeant made a mess of procedures, something about you and a phone call, it was all rather vague to me," he said. "They pressed me for information about the whereabouts of someone named Cheryl Norris. Who is she?" Derrick asked.

"No one, just go on," Frank ordered.

"The dead woman, the one they haven't identified, is believed to be linked to some drug activity, and this Miss Norris, well, is a mystery to them. But the *capitan* believes she's in Costa Rica," Derrick said.

The conversation proved the cops were in the dark, too. Cheryl was in the country and somehow involved. She was alive, that was news for him. Also, the cops might know more than they revealed to Derrick.

"Thanks, Derrick. We're through," Frank said.

"As you insist. Now, please, if you'll just tell me who in Washington you called, I can handle the reports," Derrick pressed.

"Derrick, go home," Frank urged.

"But Mr. Reardon, there are reports to do. Every time a U.S. citizen is apprehended in a foreign country we ..."

"Derrick, we're done," Frank said as he stood.

"But the reports?" Derrick protested.

"Derrick, leave!" Frank commanded.

Derrick finally understood from Frank's eyes that the conversation was terminated, and he left. Within the hour, Frank's friend in Washington would know he was back on the street.

Frank made his way back to the waterfront and the dock. He made a detour toward the fish shack where he had bought his sandwich and beer earlier. Eddie was sitting on the steps strumming his twelve-string guitar. Another rootless American living on the fruit dock, Eddie Pettigrew ran the small store and sold basic supplies to the crews of the ships coming and going.

"Yo, Frankie, your visit with *el Capitan* finished? Nice guy, that *Capitan* Ruiz. Got to admit, though, I don't travel in his circles."

Eddie had a way of cutting through a lot of stuff. He let you know he knew more than you suspected. He'd sit there all day, strumming that guitar, sometimes barely selling a beer, but never wanting for a buck. Frank was never able to figure the guy out.

"Yeah, he's a nice guy. We had tea," Frank said. "How'd you know I saw Ruiz?"

"Anybody who leaves here with the two monkeys that grabbed you goes straight to his office, common knowledge."

"Uh huh," Frank muttered. "Never had a chance to drink this beer, any chance of me swapping it for a cold one?"

"Sure, why not? Some cargo ship grunt will take your warm one. Swap it out and get me one, too. Stay a while."

"Maybe next time, Eddie, I'm in the mood for some quiet time," Frank said as he pulled a cold beer from the cooler.

Frank continued through the truckloads of cargo being moved between ships and warehouses. The head of security on the dock spotted Frank from the window of his office on the second floor of the administration building. He ran from the building, calling to Frank.

Manuel Rivera, dock *jefe*, was a slender Afro-Caribe with powerful forearms and a bald head. Rivera cut an intimidating figure on the waterfront. His personal uniform was always the same, green and black jungle camouflage pants, jump boots polished to a high shine, and a tight fitting black T-shirt that showed off a well-defined chest and his six-pack abdomen. The whole look was topped off by a sweat-stained red and black bandanna tied tightly with a double knot around his neck.

He saw his position on the dock as proof Central American people had the ability to achieve success, despite the contrarian view of investors from the United States. He worked for these people, but he also believed the Americans took an imperialist view of Costa Ricans.

The dock boss strutted around with a new Belgian-made 5.7mm automatic pistol in a hip holster. The 5.7mm, with its twenty-shot armor piercing bullets, was a tactical weapon designed for NATO assault troops. It was available only to government agencies by international treaty. How Manny, a waterfront security guard, got his hands on this gun was anyone's guess.

Manny felt the docks were his turf. He resented the freewheeling access allowed to Frank by the Americans who controlled all shipping operations through a government lease. As a result, there was ongoing tension between the two men.

During a fishing trip, Frank once asked the New York shipping company CEO who was Manny's boss where he found Manny and why he kept him around. "The guy is a thug, you know," Frank offered.

"Yeah, he is, and you'd recognize the type," the company executive laughed. "But he does get the job done."

Manny kept coming toward Frank, hollering across the compound. "Reardon, wait. I want to talk to you. You brought the *policia* to my docks this morning. I don't like that. What did they want?" he demanded.

"I didn't bring them, Manny. They came on their own," Frank said as he walked.

"It's *Senor Rivera*. Remember that, and I don't care who your *Yanqui* friends are in Nueva York. Now, tell me what I want to know," Manny said, stopping Frank.

"It was a mix-up, that's all. They thought I knew someone they were checking up on. It's nothing. Go ask them yourself," Frank said.

"Don't think I won't, *senor*," Manny countered.

Frank stopped and turned to face Manny. The two men stood steadfast, staring into each other's eyes, Frank holding his cold beer in his left hand and Manny with his right hand on the butt of the 5.7mm pistol. Then Manny blinked. The dock security chief stepped aside.

Minutes later, as Frank reached the pier leading to his boat, two men stepped out from behind a dumpster and pointed toward him, smiling.

"*Hola, muchacho*! Good to see you," one called jovially. Frank continued walking toward his boat and the men, moving a tad slower and without answering.

"*Amigo*, we've been waiting for you. Where have you been?" the second one called out.

The greeting had a tone of friendliness. Only Frank didn't know either one of the men. He closed in on his boat and attempted to pass the two strangers quietly. The younger of the two men, who was barrel-chested and much heavier than Frank, blocked his path.

"I want to talk to you, *senor*," he said softly. The sound of his voice didn't carry down the dock as much as his initial greeting.

Frank stopped and stared at him. The second man was about ten feet behind the first guy. He was slender and well built. Another ten feet behind the second man, Dutch stood on the deck growling every time one of the two men moved toward the gangplank of the boat. Frank knew nobody had yet boarded his vessel.

"What do you want?" Frank asked.

"The woman, where is she, *senor*?" asked the second man.

"What woman, who are you talking about?" Frank asked.

"Don't play with us, *senor*. I ask you nicely once more, where is the woman?"

"You have the wrong guy, *amigo*," Frank said, trying to push by him.

The man with the barrel chest grabbed Frank's arm, holding him in place, and said, "The woman in the picture. I want her. Where is she?"

Cheryl, Frank thought. *He wants Cheryl. She is in Costa Rica! And if these two clowns are looking for her, she must be connected to the murder and in trouble.*

The man tightened his grip on Frank. With one arcing swing, Frank hammered the fat man with a roundhouse punch across the bridge of his nose. Frank felt the cartilage collapse under the blow of his fist as his knuckles rolled off the man's face. The man's grip snapped open, releasing Frank's arm. Stepping in closer, Frank drove his knee into the man's groin and quickly followed up with another wallop to his temple. His victim grimaced. He was dizzy from the hits to his head. The pain left him too weak to fight back.

Frank spun around and immediately drove a left jab into the chest of the second guy charging at him. The guy rocked backwards. Before his attacker regained his balance, Frank advanced and hit his jaw with a right cross, followed by a quick left to his ribs. The attacker doubled over in agony. Frank grabbed him by the back of his shirt collar and ran him head first into a stack of empty fuel barrels on the dock, knocking him unconscious.

As fast as he could, Frank swung around. The fat man was rising to his knees and fumbling for a pistol under his shirt. Sprinting toward him, Frank kicked the man in the head. A shot rang out from the weapon as the gun bounced on the dock. Frank jumped over the fat man and kicked the gun into the water. He turned and punched the man as he tried to get on his feet.

Eddie came rushing down the dock as Frank traded punches with the thin man who had regained consciousness. With one solid upper cut to his chin, Frank sent his opponent flying off the edge of the dock and into the water.

Dutch was barking wildly. The fat man was starting to regain his footing as Eddie scooped up a bucket and flung it at his head. *El Gordo* went down again, sprawled out on his stomach, arms and feet extended, on the dock.

The fat man tried to stand up again. Frank swung away at him with two hard-hitting blows to his temple. The punches drove him back down onto his knees. He struggled to raise his rotund frame.

Frank grabbed him by the back of his collar and propelled him along the pier. Building forward momentum, he tossed the fat man onto the stern of the *Celtic Mistress.* The man fell to the deck unconscious.

Frank jumped on board and tied the man's ankles to a cleat. "Cast me off," he commanded Eddie as he fired up the engines.

"What are you doing?" Eddie yelled.

"Get the bow lines, cast me off," Frank repeated. "Hurry!" he yelled, as the twin engines roared to life. In the distance, Manny and his dock thugs came rushing toward the boat.

Eddie unleashed the last rope and jumped on board.

"Get off!" Frank hollered.

"Nope, I'm with you."

"Dutch! Here!" Frank commanded. He positioned the dog between himself and Eddie. Frank turned the wheel and pulled his boat away from the dock at full throttle. "Stay put, and Dutch won't have you for lunch."

On the dock Manny's men were busy fishing the thin guy out of the water. The dock boss glared at Frank steaming away into the Caribbean. He muttered curses in the island patois he fought to avoid in everyday speech.

On the *Celtic Mistress*, Frank muttered, too. All he wanted today was a sandwich and a beer. The men on the dock were younger and stronger, but Frank was more experienced in survival techniques. He always told rookie cops, never rely on first impressions. It's only results that count.

Three

Inside the ornate conference room of a white granite office building in Washington, a coterie of navy blue and gray suits assembled to assess a murder in Costa Rica and how it was disrupting their schedules in the capital of democracy. Each participant reviewed the mission folder before him to make sure he was free of fault. Someone was surely going to catch hell for the screw-ups leading to the murder of the woman.

Todd Hickey, a senior strategist and one of the newer members of the team, sat at the long table, attentive and nervous. He hadn't met the new director but was eager to advance his political stature in the agency and on the team. He believed by being aggressive at this gathering he could demonstrate that his years in international deployment support management had value for this new covert operations unit.

"What do we have?" asked the man at the head of the table.

No roll call was taken, and no pleasantries were exchanged. When Thomas Aikens, director of special and covert operations for Homeland Security, called a meeting, everyone invited came. No excuses were accepted. His reputation in managing clandestine operations was widely known in Washington circles.

"One asset has been eliminated, and the target product is temporarily missing," Hickey responded immediately. "However, we're optimistic that a full product recovery will occur and the operation will be back on track shortly," he offered from his seat in the middle of the long conference room table.

The man at the head of the table put down his briefing papers, peered over his half-frame glasses and sighed. "You have never been a field operative, have you?"

"No, sir, I am a senior strategist. I am required to be based here in Washington in order for me to monitor and support multiple fronts simultaneously. My responsibilities …"

"Shut up." Aikens said calmly.

"Sir?" the young man asked.

"I said, shut up. Speak again when I ask you another question."

Hickey froze. He shifted his eyes back and forth along the table without moving his head to see if any of his colleagues were reacting, or worse, snickering at the head man's denouncement. Appearances were everything in Washington.

"You're a fool," Aikens said calmly.

Hickey cleared his throat and straightened his Hermes tie.

"Let me tell you what you have going on down there," said Aikens. "You managed to get a freelancer murdered. You brought local cops into the mix and didn't control their involvement. And, as an aside, I don't like freelancers. I've used them, but sparingly and always reluctantly. They are by nature uncontrollable. Also, your freelancer wasn't properly approved, but we'll address that later."

"But you said …" Hickey tried to interrupt.

"I said have a local ally, maybe an individual cop, help monitor the situation while we re-group and assess our next steps. But no, you bring in the captain of the command, and he launches a friggin' investigation and arrests an American citizen!"

"Sir, is it so significant that some tourist took a pinch? I hear he got sprung, anyway."

"Stop," Aikens ordered as he leaned and placed his palms on the mahogany tabletop. "You really are a fool, aren't you? Have you read that tourist's file?"

"File, he has a file?" Hickey murmured.

"Yes, he has a goddamned file! He's a retired homicide cop with more than a hundred investigations and a record for clearing cases. He apparently also has a friend somewhere in the State Department who can spring him all the way from Washington with a single phone call. How many tourists have that kind of influence?"

"Who's the friend?" someone else asked.

"Good question, find out!"

"Sir, closing local police cases? Is that really relevant?" Hickey pressed, hoping to recapture his position with the group.

"I think so. Remember that congressman from Connecticut killed a few years ago? That was his case. He cleared that case in six weeks and caught the stalker who was trying to frame the congressman's widow. He was, in my opinion, tenacious and relentless in the case."

"He's still just a street cop. I think we should be on guard against overreacting to his involvement. Why are we so concerned? He's retired. He's hung up his shield," Hickey retorted after a quick skimming of the file before him.

"What is your name?"

"Todd Hickey, sir. I was just transferred over to this unit from the State Department's Central American desk," Hickey said. "I was in deployment support management."

The boss ignored the young man's resume chatter and said, "Interesting observation, Mr. Hickey. The only problem with your analysis is that he's on the street down there while you people are up here. He's in his world, not bouncing off the walls in Washington."

As the new head of this clandestine group, Aikens needed a more complete picture of Frank Reardon. He needed to know who this man was and what motivated him. The intelligence chief knew the young team in front of him wasn't equipped to deal with the challenges Reardon posed for the assembled group. Aikens needed ground troops, people who had the ability and drive to function in a manner fueled only by their surroundings.

Looking over the assembled group, Aikens made eye contact with the team psychologist. "Doc, is he a threat to us? What do you think he's capable of down there?"

"I can't assess this man with so little information," the profiler said.

"Assess this point for me, sir. On his last case he was lured into chasing a perp who killed a store cashier. The perp ran down an alley and hid in the shadows. It was a ruse. Our boy was off duty having a drink in the bar next door. When our street cop turned down the alley, the perp

let loose with two rounds, hitting him in the chest and
putting him in the hospital for six weeks. While he was
lying on the ground bleeding, the shooter took his wallet,
went to his home and killed his wife with two more shots.
He left the pistol on the kitchen table with the last two
rounds still in it. This cop's wife was buried before he was
out of the hospital. He retired after that, but personally, I
think he just left a job. Now, what do you say?"

"I still can't assess him properly," the doctor
maintained.

"Doc, consider this," the boss pressed, "he was laid up
in a hospital when his wife was killed, and now he's on his
feet while another woman is being threatened. Quick, give
me an answer, a gut reaction. How do you think he's going
to react?"

Under pressure, the doctor said, "Well, he could be
clinically depressed to the point where he wants to just
hole up or …" and at this point, the doctor paused.

"Or what, doc?" Aikens continued.

"Well, considering his background, he could be a very
dangerous man. He may feel he has nothing to lose and
therefore nothing to fear from anything or anyone. In that
case his actions are limited only by his personal sense of
justice, which may or may not dovetail with any
recognized authority."

"In other words, the ultimate free agent," Aikens said.

"Yes, in layman's language, that would be accurate,"
the doctor said.

"Thank you. Now who wants to bet he'll just disappear
quietly?" The group was silent. "Let's assess, as to our
friends …"

"Friends?" someone asked.

"Yes, in addition to our so-called tourist, we have to consider your police pal, remember him? Did you know Captain Guillermo Ruiz is part of a prominent family in Costa Rica?"

There were blank stares all around the table, the unspoken answer he had anticipated. "I guess not," he said disparagingly. "Who ran this operation, Moe, Larry and Curly?" He looked down at his briefing papers and shook his head. *Amateurs*, he thought to himself, *every one of them Ivy League children, not a functioning operative in the group.* "Let's make this man our friend and do it fast," he said, going back to his papers. "Let's try to get on point. We went down there to plant misinformation inside the Central American network of drug dealers and runners, correct?"

Heads nodded in agreement all around the table.

"So somehow a woman not part of our plan got killed, and another woman, also not part of the plan, is now involved and on the run. And our bulldog of a cop, also not part of the plan, has entered the chase?" Heads around the table again nodded in agreement. "What is left of this operation that we control?" There was no response, and the attendees started anxiously shuffling the papers before them on the table.

The boss shook his head in disbelief. "Specifically, it was our intention to funnel to the Central American drug networks fake U.S. Coast Guard patrol schedules. We would do this by leaking to them computerized access to a fictitious government database, correct?" Heads nodded yet again. "This information was geared to push them into travel patterns we could track and use to design interdiction procedures, still correct?"

"Yes, sir," a voice at the table said. "The Central American *cocaineros* work for the South American drug cartels that are more sophisticated and savvy."

"And presumably less likely to be fooled," the director remarked. "I am wondering who turned out to be the fool here. So, continuing, this information was to be leaked to them through a small-time American drug dealer we flipped into being an operative for us?"

"That's correct," another voice said.

"And this access comes through a computer disc? Someone explain."

"Well, sir, the disc was designed to appear as if it was a government product giving the holder access to databases housing information about Coast Guard patrols and routes," Hickey chimed in. "Actually, it accesses an old government network decommissioned by us. The network was a known entity in certain circles, and by reputation, carried believability. It was something we could co-opt into being an electronic Trojan horse for our needs. If the drug traffickers believed they were able to access U.S. government networks and secure information on American patrols, we believed we could direct their movements with the misinformation in a way that worked to our advantage. That is the point where we felt, if they took the bait, we could plan interdiction actions against them," Hickey explained.

"God, you sound like a bureaucrat," Aikens said. "So, how were the operatives selected?"

"The word was put out by the FBI through the Department of Justice for U.S. Attorneys to be on the lookout for potential candidates, low- to mid-level dealers under indictment looking to make sweetheart deals with the authorities. Once the FBI locked in on a guy, we funneled him through our undercover people to the drug rings in Central America," a team member said.

"This was initially an FBI project, correct?" he asked.

"Yes, sir," someone answered.

"And what controls did you have on this operative?"

"He was to make daily calls to a secure phone."

"And why would the traffickers in Central America believe some low- to mid-level dope dealer in the States would have access to technology allowing him to tap into government databases?"

"We established that one of his customers was a government computer analyst," someone said.

"Who?"

"A fictitious person. We planted employment histories in the right files and then killed him off, so to speak. We had obituaries published in local newspapers. It made verifying the network impossible. Everything was timed to coincide with our operative receiving the disc," another said.

"What was his support, backup in the field?"

"Not necessary, he was only tasked with inserting the disc with the target group and getting out. He was ordered to phone in daily."

"Really? And where is he now?"

"Uh, he appears to be missing, but we think only for the moment."

"He's dead, you idiot! Just like your friend over there," Aikens said pointing to Hickey, "I can see you've never been a field operative, either. I can't believe you put a freelancer in the field without backup and only the hope he'd make a daily phone call."

"Why do you think he's dead, sir?" a new voice asked.

"Years of experience and the obvious stupidity of this plan!" he hollered. "Has anyone identified the dead girl yet?"

"We're working on it."

"She's probably a girlfriend to your missing asset. Identify her and verify her role. We have a lot of details to fill in," he said. "It looks like the FBI handed this mess off to us as soon as it turned sour."

The assembled team before him now sat sheepishly in silence. The operation had gone bad, and they knew it.

"Where's the disc now?" he finally asked.

"We don't know, sir," a voice offered.

"Finally, a straight answer," he said. "The bad guys believe the disc is real, and the odds are the other woman has it or knows where it is located, right?"

"Yes."

"Is there any chance we've developed any leads to identify her?"

"Not yet, boss," a voice offered.

"Wonderful, I'll bet our retired cop from Bridgeport has already identified her, and she's the reason he's involved."

Finally, one senior member in the room rose to modulate the growing tension.

"Maybe now is a good time for a brief break," Martin Greco, operations supervisor of the unit, said to the group. "Mr. Director, I have something here that needs your confidential attention," he said to Aikens.

Greco pulled Aikens out of the room and into the hall so he could cool off. The two men strolled to a window that looked out over the Washington Mall. They stood in silence, gazing at the rectangular expanse of grass below. Greco knew his friend well enough to stay quiet for a moment longer. His friend's mind was silently mulling the issues and formulating appropriate actions.

Tom always found it calming to scan the stretch of Washington grass starting at the base of the Capitol building, past the solitary Washington Monument, and then beyond to the Lincoln Memorial. *The mall really is America's lawn,* he thought. Others rushed to the oceans or the mountains for peace and quiet. Not Tom Aikens. Washington was where he found solace, watching the wheels of government slowly grind forward. Unfortunately, when one of those wheels became stuck, or the tooth of a gear broke, it was often his job to jump in and make a rapid, and always silent, repair.

Aikens had been handling black operations within various government agencies for years. He had experience with some of the nation's most difficult and sensitive intelligence and security matters. When he was asked to become the director of the new classified International Security Intelligence Unit under Homeland Security, he insisted upon and received complete operational control. He demanded his position be a direct report to both the Secretary of Homeland Security and the President. The dual level of reporting gave him a guarantee that any voice of opposition to one of his plans would be heard in the Oval Office. Aikens was known as a tough team leader in the field who got the job done and done quietly. It wasn't always so, however.

Back in 1980 as a young Army intelligence officer, Aikens attended a classified meeting at the White House headed by President Jimmy Carter. The President was on the verge of authorizing a mission concocted to free some fifty-four Americans held hostage by Iranian militants at the U.S. Embassy in Tehran. The mission, as planned to that point, involved a commando team being dropped into the desert, making their way in secret into the city, rescuing the Americans, and being extracted by helicopters to a safe haven in nearby Oman.

The rescue date had already been set for April, even though many of the mission details were still hypothetical. Aikens sat there listening to senior officers argue that the mission tactics were poorly planned. He distinctly remembered one officer saying the equipment being considered for the rescue wasn't reliable.

Aikens' assignment was to devise a route for the extraction team to travel from the desert through the city to the embassy and then, after the rescue was over, to a soccer field for pickup by the choppers. He wanted more time to develop backup routes, in the event of some unforeseen development. Carter's political people deemed that a waste of time. The element of surprise was more of an edge than was needed.

"The streets and alleys of Tehran aren't like moving across the open expanse of the desert," he protested. "One disabled truck in a narrow street, whether it's there by accident or placed there deliberately, leaves us pinned down like sitting ducks. And we'll be moving fifty-four unarmed and possibly weak or injured American civilians."

"Soldier, just do your job," he was told. Aikens was dismayed by the decision, especially considering Carter was a naval officer.

In the end, the President, pushed by the political wonks in the White House, approved the mission. The Tehran rescue mission was launched in April and ended in disaster. Choppers were late arriving at the rendezvous point; one bird was scrubbed because of a mechanical breakdown, another chopper crashed. The mission was ultimately cancelled and an air strike was called in to destroy the equipment and munitions delivered to the Iranian desert outside Tehran. No embassy hostages were ever rescued.

Somewhere in the attic of his Maryland home, Aikens still had his original route maps, the ones he never had a chance to use.

There was plenty of blame to go around after the Tehran mission failed. Aikens took his lumps and privately swore that going forward he'd always strive to be in control or not involved at all.

"This is a real mess, Tom," Greco said, bringing the intelligence chief back to the present. "We inherited a ticking bomb from the FBI."

"You're right, and we'll deal with the politics and the blame game at a later date. Right now we've got one dead body, probably a second that hasn't popped up yet. We need to regain operational control."

"Agreed, but that may be a tall order," Greco said.

"We have a choice?" the director asked rhetorically.

"You have some ideas?"

"Better yet, I may have someone on the ground nearby who might be able to help," the boss said.

Greco stared at him. "Who?" he asked.

"Let's just say that after I was stung by the mess in the desert under the Carter administration, I decided never to be without an insurance policy again."

Greco had known Aikens as long as he'd known anyone in Washington. He understood.

"It's a safe bet the FBI's operative was killed up here after he made a connection with the bad guys. Something went wrong with the deal," Aikens said, "and probably after a *cocainero* paid some serious money for the disc.

"Makes sense," Greco agreed. "Even the FBI wouldn't let someone under indictment that they flipped leave the country. That's too much heat to deal with if things went bad. If he was killed stateside, well, to the FBI he'd just be another dealer who turned up dead. They'd just move on. So following your theory, he was killed because the disc was never actually delivered to them."

"Right, but the woman stepped in somehow, snatched the disc, and she was lured or went down to Costa Rica voluntarily," Aikens said. "Only things became worse. The disc is still in the wind, and the bad guys still believe in it. After this point, I'm lost. You believe the new woman and the cop are complete wild cards and not in any way part of the original scheme whatsoever?" Aikens asked.

"Yes, but yet they are also somehow connected to each other," Greco said. "Let's get back inside."

"I'll be in momentarily. Get everyone settled down, Marty."

Aikens looked across the mall on an angle and stared at the White House on Pennsylvania Avenue. Very few of the men who ever lived there understood his work fully. For the most part, presidents made political decisions. In the field, decisions were made on things more basic. Survival and mission control usually topped the list of factors to consider.

In his mind Aikens compartmentalized the issues facing him now. The unknown woman probably had the disc. He had to find her and deal with her. He also had to find Frank Reardon and get some control over him, too. Aikens shook his head. The girl, Reardon and the targeted drug gangs were the only remaining players and he didn't control any of them. He scratched the back of his neck to ease a tightening muscle. So many questions, Aikens thought. He hated playing catch up. Poor planning wasn't going to cost him lives again. This mission was still doable.

He was sure the recruit put in the field was dead. If his body was ever found, it might produce some forensic evidence. Others would have to worry about that later. Aikens' primary focus was to gain mission control and find both Reardon and the mystery woman.

He returned to the conference room. Greco cleared his throat loudly enough to command silence and nodded at Aikens, standing at the table.

The director outlined a plan of identifying and locating the woman, ascertaining the status of the disc, and finding Frank Reardon. Simultaneously, control of the operation needed to be obtained immediately. The attendees took notes feverishly as Aikens barked orders to different people. He demanded more frequent updates and tightened lines of communication between himself and Greco and the team. Then he dismissed them.

The team gathered up their papers and headed out. Aikens ignored the suits as they passed by him until the strategist approached the door. Without looking up from his papers, Aikens reached out and grabbed Todd's arm as he passed by the edge of the table.

"Mr. Hickey, you're going to Costa Rica," Aikens said.

"Me?"

"Yes, liaise with Derrick Hines, and don't acknowledge anyone from this team unless they approach you first, got it? If you encounter someone, treat them like a stranger. You don't have opening line privileges. Do as you're told by Hines or someone from this team."

"Sir, I think my contributions have more value …"

"Hickey, I will determine the value of your services and where and how they will be used by this team. You leave tonight. You're dismissed," he said.

The young man said nothing as he left the room.

"You think that's a good idea?" Greco asked.

"It gets him out of my way. He'll be based in San Jose on the Pacific side of the country. The operation is centered on the Caribbean side around Limon," Aikens said. "Besides, isn't Hines, the embassy guy down there, the guy who actually spoke with Reardon, isn't he the son of Sen. Robert Hines?"

"Yes, he is," Greco answered.

"Good, send the Senator a note that we appreciate his son's help and discretion in dealing with a person of interest in one of our matters. Tell him we're sending his son a new assistant, even though it may only be on a temporary basis. The politician in him will get a charge out of being loosely connected to an intelligence matter," Aikens said. "While you're at it, find out who Hickey's patron is here in Washington. He didn't get here through a civil service test. We'll want to cover that political base, too, making it look like we're utilizing the young man in a serious way."

Greco smiled, wondering who the bigger politician was in this mission.

"Boss?" an aide interrupted as he broke into the conference room.

"What?" the big man snapped back.

"Your cop, the guy we've been tracking? Well, we just got word he snatched a bad guy. He's heading out with him into the open water of the Caribbean Sea on a fishing boat."

Aikens looked at Greco and shook his head.

The profiler had been lingering in the rear of the conference room. As he approached the door he overheard the announcement.

Aikens looked at him and calmly asked, "Doc, any opinions now about whether he's depressed or dangerous?"

Four

Out on the water Frank scanned the horizon for chase boats. There didn't seem to be anyone following him, at least not yet. He squinted tightly and still saw nothing. At least for the moment, he had time to think.

Frank killed the engines and let the boat drift. He took a roll of duct tape off a ledge by the ship's wheel and looked over at his captive. He wrapped his prisoner's wrists and tore off another six-inch strip and sealed his mouth.

"You think you need to keep him that quiet out here?" Eddie chuckled.

Frank looked over at him and said nothing. Eddie hadn't moved since he was told to stay put, and neither had Dutch. Frank tied the fat man's ankles with the rope tangled up at his feet. He checked the heading of his vessel and kept it on autopilot straight out into the Caribbean. His prisoner was starting to regain consciousness in the open sea air.

"Let's you and me talk," Frank said, turning to Eddie. "What are you doing here?"

"What do you mean?" he asked innocently.

"Cut the crap, I drop two goons on the dock as Manny comes rushing down the planks. I take off with one on my boat, and you just jump on for the ride? And how'd you know I was with Captain Ruiz?"

"Come on; give me a break, will you? Heel this dog and we can talk."

"I can hear you just fine with Dutch right where he is," Frank said calmly. "Funny thing about dogs, most people fear them more than a gun or a knife. Don't you agree? You've obeyed my commands exactly and never given Dutch any cause to react. It's like you understand how to use dogs, too. Am I right?" Frank said.

Eddie didn't move. He smiled slightly to indicate he agreed with Frank. "Come on, man, everyone has a past. We don't need to dig around in histories," he offered, trying to buy some time and assess his options. "I mean, when the cops picked you up this morning and you said you wanted to phone a friend to feed this hound, I never told anyone you called someone in Washington. That call got you sprung, right?"

Frank chuckled. "Digging around in past histories is exactly what we're going to do. Even the cops didn't know I called Washington until I told them. How did you know? You either checked with the international operator or that phone in your shack is wired up somehow," Frank said as he slowly drew a revolver out from underneath the ship's wheel. "I'm waiting."

Eddie shook his head. He fell right into Frank's trap.

"Man, you're tense. OK, truth time, but I don't know much," he said. "I sorta watch out for things for people. You know, comings and goings, that sort of thing," he said.

"Details," Frank said coldly.

"I'm a little short on details. I got a call a few days ago from some people to be on the lookout for something involving a transaction between an American and some of the drug running gangs down here," he said.

"Who called?" Frank asked.

"No. That you don't get," Eddie said, "but they're our people."

Frank cocked the pistol.

"Use it if you want, man. I'll talk, but names you don't get," Eddie said.

Frank released the hammer and simply said, "Continue."

"All I know is that there was some sort of drug deal back home in the U.S., some guy went missing, and a chick was here to complete the deal. I was to try and locate any of the principals and assess what they were up to and report back. Then the cops grabbed you, and word has it the chick is dead and some other woman is involved," Eddie said. "I figured you were the only real lead to follow, so when the dock fight erupted, I saw it as a chance to get into this thing. You dropped both guys and pulled this water escape. And here we are."

Frank just stared at him. Eddie started to inch closer, and Dutch growled. Frank snapped to attention. "Going somewhere?"

"Come on, man! You got the dog, the gun, we're out here all alone. My legs are stiff."

"Who?" Frank asked.

"Nope, no names. That's a deal breaker," Eddie said.

Frank continued to stare at Eddie and then relented. He had the information he needed. Eddie was a player, an agent of some sort, probably a freelancer. He knew Eddie's bosses would surface sooner or later.

"Satisfied?" Eddie asked.

"For now. We'll talk again," Frank said. "Just to be fair, here's my piece of this mess. The cops hauled me in about the death of a woman they believed to be Cheryl Norris, someone I knew years ago. Only the body they have isn't Cheryl. The dead woman had Cheryl's identification papers. They cut me loose after I proved they had the wrong name on their body and I had no connection to the dead woman. Now it seems that Cheryl is in Costa Rica and somehow involved," Frank said. "I need to find her and help her out of this mess, whatever it is."

"And that call to Washington?" Eddie asked.

"Just a friend who was able to cut through the bureaucracy and tell Ruiz to charge me or release me, that's all," he said.

"Nice friend, who is he?" Eddie pressed.

"Forget it," Frank answered.

Eddie shrugged. He tried. "Now what?" he asked.

"It's chit-chat time for my friend here. I want to see how much he knows," Frank said. As he approached his captive, he pulled a machete out from under some tarps in the rear of the boat. The man stared up at him with no emotion in his eyes. He didn't fear Frank, even though he was hogtied and defenseless.

Frank smiled as he approached the man, blade in hand. "I need some answers, *amigo*," he said, ripping the tape off his mouth.

His captive was unresponsive, ignoring the pain of the tape being removed.

Frank grabbed his bound wrist and yanked him to his feet. He raised the machete in the air. "I really think we should talk," he said.

Still, his captive showed no response. Then the man smiled and said, "*No ingles.*"

"No English, huh? Too bad. Well, too bad for you, *amigo.*"

Slowly, Frank lowered the blade toward the man. At the last moment, he twisted the blade, dull side down, and slid the machete between his tied wrists. He let the dull end just drop against the tape that bound his hands together.

The captive smiled. *This weak gringo doesn't have the stomach to use the weapon,* he thought.

Frank stared into his eyes and smiled again. He turned the blade inward toward his captive's left hand and drew it across his fleshy palm. Blood oozed immediately. He brought the blade to a stop when it was at the halfway point on his palm. He flipped the sharpened edge to his captive's other palm and split his flesh again. The salty sweat on his captive's two hands burned the open wounds but not enough to make the man flinch.

"*Yanqui mujer,*" he growled at Frank.

"Funny, very funny," Frank said. The former cop pushed aside some rods and reels and found three buckets of warm chum. One by one he dumped the bloody swill from the buckets overboard. The sea alongside the boat turned red and then the mush congealed into a black mess. "See, if you were a fisherman, you'd know we were in Shark Alley."

The captive twisted his body around and looked out into the water.

"Here they come," Frank said, pointing to a couple of dorsal fins about a hundred yards off the starboard side of the Celtic Mistress. He grabbed the man by the scruff of the neck and dragged him over to the edge of the boat and dipped his bloody palms into the water. "They like snacks, *amigo*, first fingers, then hands, arms and whatever follows. Piss me off anymore and they'll get all of you," he said coldly.

The man twisted his head up and looked at Frank. Then he looked at a fin coming right at him. Looking up at Frank again, he saw only two cold, unflinching eyes. The captive knew all about Shark Alley.

"Yeah, you know what that is out there, don't you?" Frank said as the dorsal fin stopped circling and started to swim toward the boat. "You know damn well it's a bull shark, a big fat, dumb ugly beast that eats anything it can sink its teeth into, right? You've watched these sharks since you were a kid, fat man," Frank said.

"A bull shark?" Eddie asked from behind.

"Yeah, it's a man-eater, and anything else it can find in the water. They're big, stupid and deadly, and this guy knows all about them," Frank said, wiggling the man's body so the fresh blood from his hands spread through the water. Frank leaned over the fat man and heard him starting to gasp for air.

The shark was closing in on the boat, slowly weaving left and right, assessing what was spilling blood in its feeding waters. Cursed with poor sight, the bull shark tracked vibrations in the water. The shark gobbled up whatever it could find, instantly and roughly shredding the captured prey in its huge mouth that was lined with razor sharp teeth. The beast was indiscriminate and graceless. The fish broke the water, and his tail popped up. About eight feet long, dull grey in color, bulky, with eyes set back deep in its head, all in all an ugly animal.

The thug was in terror as Frank gave him a shake at the neck while he was humped over the back end of the boat at the waist. The fat man knew all about the bull sharks along the coast of Costa Rica. Since he was a kid, hustling sea shells to tourists on the beach, he had seen the pain they inflicted on people. The sharks were drawn into shallow waters by scraps of food and swimmers splashing in the waves.

"Here he comes," Frank said.

The captive let out a scream. Dutch jumped a bit as the sound of the man's voice disappeared over the water.

"Please, please," he begged. "I'll talk with you, please!" he screeched. "Pull me up!"

Frank yanked the man's bloody hands from the water just as the shark swam by and bumped the boat. He bent him back over the rail and back into the water as the fish went by and dove under the boat. "Will we have to repeat this?"

"No, no, I'll talk, I'll talk, I'll talk!" he screamed.

"Who do you work for?" Frank asked.

The man was silent. Frank edged toward him, but he stopped when the man said loudly "Mendoza, I do jobs for Mendoza."

"Oh, great, Mendoza," Eddie said. "You've got a Felix Mendoza guy here. Mendoza is one of the biggest, if not the biggest, drug runner around. They call him Felix behind his back. He was given the nickname because he always has a bag of tricks, like the cartoon character Felix the Cat, to protect himself. His real name is Raul Cordova Mendoza," Eddie said, "and he's not a nice guy. He's very tight with the Colombians. And another thing, that other guy you dropped on the dock, by now he's back in some

Mendoza compound giving him the rundown on you, me and this boat. They'll be after us pretty soon. Boy, when you pick a fight, you don't screw around," Eddie said.

Frank ignored Eddie. "Let's talk about the dead woman, who is she? And where is Cheryl Norris?" he asked the fat man.

The man wrung his bleeding hands.

"The dead woman came here to sell Mendoza information about American Coast Guard patrols. Her boyfriend met with Mendoza's people in *los Estados Unidos*. The *gringo* tried to trick them into paying more money for the information. I am told he paid a price, a deadly price. His *mujer* tried the same trick here in Costa Rica, I think. Mendoza became angry and ordered her to be killed. I was not there when it happened." he said.

"Cheryl Norris, where is she?" Frank demanded.

"I do not know this woman," he said.

Frank glared at him and grabbed the bindings around his wrists and started to drag him to the edge of the boat.

"No, no, wait! Her name, I do not know this name, but there was another woman!" he whimpered.

"You might want to listen to him a bit more," Eddie offered from behind.

"Shut up!" Frank commanded. "You," he said, turning back to his prisoner, "keep talking."

"There was another woman, I never saw her. She took the information that was promised to Mendoza from a hiding place set up by the dead woman. Mendoza only wants what he was promised!" he screamed.

Frank stepped back.

"Now what, pal? You got two dead bodies, and your friend is still on the lam," Eddie said.

"I said, shut up!" Frank hollered.

"Who is looking for this woman? Where are they now?" he asked his captive.

"I only help Mendoza's regular men. I just pick up a little work here and there. Paco, the other man on the dock, and me, get jobs off and on from Mendoza's people. Usually we just have to scare people," the man said.

"Where will Mendoza look for her?" Frank asked coldly.

"I don't know," he said. The man stared at Frank and the machete. His hands were still stinging from the salt of his sweat and the water. "Up and down the coast there are people Mendoza pays to watch the comings and goings of strangers, not tourists, people who don't belong. You were watched for a while, too," he said. "Mendoza has many people on his payroll. He'll go to them."

"I want a list," Frank said, "a list, or you go into the water with the fish."

The man nodded quickly, and Frank gave him a towel to wrap around his bleeding hands and a pen and a paper bag to write his list.

"You know this Mendoza?" Frank asked Eddie.

"I know he's not a guy to mess with, I know that much," he said.

"You in or out?" Frank asked.

"In or out of what? You're not seriously thinking of taking on Mendoza, are you?"

"I'm going after the woman, she's a friend. I have to find her. If Mendoza gets in the way, well, I'll deal with that at the time," Frank said.

"I wouldn't be so cavalier about Mendoza. And, what are you going to do, just drift in and out of villages up and down the coastline looking for an American woman on the run? Yeah, I can see a lot of *mestizos* rushing out to help you with that one," Eddie said.

"I asked you before, you in or out? If you have any suggestions, now is a good time to speak up," Frank said.

"I say we wait and see what Mendoza does, follow his lead to the woman," Eddie offered.

"No, that puts him in charge. I'd rather have him chasing me than leading me around in circles."

"It won't be a very long chase if he catches you messing in his business," Eddie said. "And what about this clown?" he said, pointing to the fat man, still bound and bleeding from the palms. "What about him?"

Frank looked at his captive and pondered the options.

"I have an idea," Frank said. He fired up the engines of the *Celtic Mistress* and turned the boat north along the coastline. A little later, he slowed the engines and slipped the boat into a low-hanging fog bank. He planned to dump *el gordo* in the water near one of the fishing villages along the shore.

The sun was setting and it was getting dark on the water. The boat's profile was almost invisible from shore. Finally Frank pointed to a village dock in the distance and said, "There, we'll head over there!"

Eddie leaned over and said to Frank, "Mendoza will kill this guy if he finds out he talked to you. Are you that cold-hearted? He doesn't deserve a bullet from Mendoza. The guy is just local muscle."

"You're right, and I've thought about that."

He killed the engines again and let the boat drift to about fifty yards off shore. Turning to the fat man he said, "My friend here said Mendoza will kill you if he believes you talked to me."

The man nodded, "*Es verdad*. He will."

"So, here's what you say: We fought, I came after you with a machete—the slices on your hands will prove that—and you jumped overboard. Keep it simple and you'll be fine. It's the only choice you have. Just keep it simple. If you get the chance, disappear for a while." The fat man considered what Frank said and nodded. He had no other choice. Frank cut him loose with the blade. "Now, over the side," Frank ordered.

The fat man looked at him and looked at the water. It was his only chance at staying alive, so he jumped. Frank counted to twenty after the splash, fired up the engines again, and took off once more into the Caribbean night.

"So, you think this woman you know is wired into the drug trade?" Eddie asked over the sound of the engines.

"It's been years since I've seen or spoken to her. I can't believe she's in the drug trade. There's something else going on here," Frank said. "Either way, I have to find her and find out."

"People change," Eddie offered.

"Maybe, but I doubt this one changed that much. Not her," Frank insisted. "One of the names on the fat man's list is someone I know. Maybe we can get him to help us make sense of this mess. Here, you take a look at the list. Do you know any of them?"

Eddie just stood there while Frank, holding the list of names, extended his arm without looking at him. Finally Frank looked up, then at Dutch, back to Eddie.

"Heel," Frank commanded, and the dog relaxed for the first time since the boat left the dock and curled up in a corner.

"Hell of a dog," Eddie said sarcastically.

Dutch was a true junkyard dog. He had become part of Frank's life just before he was to be put down. The animal used to belong to an old man who ran a body shop near the docks in Bridgeport. When the old guy was forced into retirement by his family, it was clear Dutch didn't fit into a world of front lawns and two-car garages. The family wanted to send Dutch off to the pound and a certain death.

The old man prevailed upon Frank to adopt Dutch. He saw the two of them as lonely souls in need of a second chance at life. Frank and the dog bonded. Dutch learned to take care of Frank, and along the way, Frank learned to rely on Dutch.

"Yeah, he is a cute little pup," Frank laughed, stepping over the dog to give Eddie the paper list of names. "We'll go to the village of San Sebastian and check out a few things. We can quietly get some supplies there, too," he said.

Eddie looked at him and said, "You play this shuffling, beer-drinking Yankee *pensionado* on the docks, but you really are a cold mother, aren't you?"

"That bothers you?" Frank asked.

Five

Frank piloted the *Celtic Mistress* up the coast in the dark toward San Sebastian village, a place he could hide for a while. He wanted to keep the boat both handy and out of sight from Mendoza's crew. Slowly heading north, he assessed other collections of shacks on the shore. None of them suited his needs. Steadily and slowly he continued to steam north, trying not to attract any attention.

"There!" he said. The village of San Sebastian was ahead. It had a nice marina known to offer basic boating services. This was an easy place to blend in and get lost.

Eddie stared at the village. It was a string of shacks identical to the other villages the *Celtic Mistress* had sailed by earlier in the night. He was befuddled trying to figure out what Reardon was thinking or planning. The former cop still hadn't shared very much.

"I know people here. We can regroup and figure things out," Frank said.

"What do you want me to do?" asked Eddie.

"Just stay handy. I want to dock this boat quietly and get some rest in the town. There are a lot of fishing boats similar to this one around here," Frank said. "The best place to hide a tree is in a forest."

"Gotcha," Eddie responded.

Frank slowed the engines and slid the *Celtic Mistress* backwards in between two other cabin cruisers. He locked up all the hatches and pulled tarps over everything before him in the wheelhouse. He hung one tarp over the stern to hide the name of the boat. Frank tossed a duffel bag onto the planks and finished tying up the boat to the dock. He spotted a trash can and fished out some empty beer bottles and assorted trash and threw it on the tarps. It all added to the appearance of the vessel being moored and forgotten.

"Let's go," Frank said, picking up his duffel bag. "Walk slowly, like you've been around here before. Look comfortable."

Eddie was just confused. The two men strolled up to the marina's lunch shack. They sat at a table and took in their surroundings. A kid brought two beers and left without taking any particular note of them. Eddie sat quietly.

"I know his father," Frank said. "When I'm sure it's safe, I'll go up and speak to him about leaving the boat here. Let's talk a bit, quietly."

Eddie was amazed. Frank was calm and cool in the face of being chased by drug dealers. He had to know the guy he cut up and dumped overboard was running straight back to Mendoza. Eventually, Mendoza's men would surface again, only better prepared. Finally, Eddie leaned over the table and said, "OK, you're in charge. I'm along for the ride. What now?"

"We have a beer, catch our breath, and enjoy the sun. These moments may become fewer and fewer going forward," he said.

The two men settled down at the old picnic table under a ratty umbrella and felt the sun warm their bodies. "Tell me about the woman," Eddie said softly.

Frank looked over at him and said nothing. He dropped his hand down to the side of the chair and unconsciously scratched Dutch behind his ear. Eddie's request was straightforward and without emotion. Finally, after deliberating to himself, he said, "Well, I guess I owe you that much."

He shared with Eddie his story of Cheryl, the summer they spent together along the Connecticut coast and the lives of two people who simply drifted apart. "Maybe it was an early love, one that never fully materialized," Frank speculated. "I don't know," he said. "I dated her years ago. Even after we parted ways, I always considered her a friend. Like I said, we went different ways." Frank was on a roll now. He spoke about his life as a cop in Bridgeport, getting married to Susan and ultimately losing her to a madman.

Eddie said nothing, he just listened. He was seeing Frank differently now as he spoke. The coldness disappeared. Sitting with him now was a vulnerable man, someone alone in the world. He was a man who had endured a great loss and was adrift.

"This bastard put two rounds into me and left me there in an alley to die. While I was lying in a pool of my own blood, the son of a bitch steals my wallet, goes to my home and kills my wife. He puts two into her at close range and leaves the goddamned gun on the table. What kind of a message is that?" he asked. "You tell me."

Frank's eyes were tearing up, but he caught himself and regained his steely look. It was too late. Eddie saw a side of Frank few ever witnessed. He knew that behind those tears this man held a commitment to extract revenge for Susan's death someday.

"And they never caught this guy?" he asked.

"Nope, he just vanished. There was never a whiff of him. The gun was wiped clean, no trace evidence to follow. It's a cold case now."

"You know he's still out there, don't you?" Eddie asked.

"Yep, and so am I," Frank said.

"And you know it was personal," Eddie continued.

"As personal as it gets. I know that, and he knows it, too. Someday I will find him," Frank predicted, "and then he's mine."

"He's waiting, you know," Eddie offered.

"Yes, I know." The coldness, the driven look, was back, and once again Frank was focused. Whatever happened in Connecticut had to keep. "I know I have something to settle back home," Frank said.

The word settle was too strong, Eddie thought. The things Frank faced could never be simply settled, the debt was too high. However, he knew Frank had to bring the matter to a conclusion. Eddie had met men like Frank before, and they were all very dangerous.

"Right now, though, I need to find Cheryl," Frank said.

The two men strolled into town. Their dirty clothes, casual demeanor, and canine companion allowed them to mix right into the small crowds of the village.

"Over there," Frank said, pointing across the street.

A three-story white cinder block building stood on the edge of the village square. It had a wooden canopy jutting out over the front entrance, and painted in crude black block letters was the word *Hotel*. Next to the hotel was a smaller building with the word *Bar* over the entrance and posters for *Presidente* beer and Havana Club rum plastered on the side of the stucco walls. On the other side of the hotel was a series of shops for tradesmen, the men who worked on the fishing boats tied up in the boatyard. There were several aging pickup trucks parked by the curb outside the buildings, and chickens ran wildly through the streets. Men unencumbered by regular jobs sat outside the buildings in the square. They passed the day making conversation with young women on the street. Some of the women were dressed in short, tight, flowered dresses and others in tight, hip-hugging pants and low-cut blouses. All of them kept glancing over to the hotel while they spoke in the hopes of enticing a customer.

Frank walked up the three steps leading to the portico on the front of the hotel. The single door leading into the square, unassuming building had a dirty glass pane in the center that had turned gray with age. Frank twisted the rusty doorknob and opened the door. He entered a long, dirty hallway illuminated by three single electric light bulbs hanging down from the ceiling spaced about ten feet apart. Dutch and Eddie followed cautiously behind in silence. On the left was a narrow counter and window with an iron grate that separated the management from the visitors. Over the bars at the window was a sign that simply read *Informacion*.

To the right of the hall was a set of French doors covered with yellowing lace curtains that opened into a formal lobby parlor. There was a bar in the corner. A metal gate was pulled down in front of the liquor bottles and dusty glassware.

"We have a cocktail hour on special occasions," a voice said from behind the guest information counter.

Frank ignored the suggestion the ancient hotel might ever host a special occasion. He paid for two rooms.

"We need to get some sleep," Frank said.

"*Mujers?*" the clerk asked.

"*No mujers, amigo,*" Frank answered.

"*Dos y tres,*" the man said, pointing upstairs and putting two keys on the counter.

"Get some sleep, I'll come for you in a few hours," Frank instructed Eddie.

"What if I take off?"

"That's your call, I don't care. If you stay, you're part of this. If you go, you're on your own. I figure we have a better chance against this Mendoza if we're together. I don't have the energy to babysit you and do what I have to do. So in a few hours, I'll know if you're in or out," he said, taking one of the keys.

"You don't have many friends, do you?" Eddie asked.

"Let's just say that has been a commodity in short supply recently in my life."

Eddie shook his head.

Frank saw the reaction and sighed. "Come over here," he said.

In the aging and dusty formal sitting room of the hotel, out of sight of the hotel clerk and people on the street, Frank reached into his duffel bag and pulled out a blue steel revolver. He handed it to Eddie.

"Keep this with you. Don't flash it around."

Eddie looked at the weapon, checked to confirm it was loaded, wrapped it in his sweatshirt and wedged it under his arm.

"Are we going steady now?" he wisecracked.

"Don't be a smart ass."

"Why the gun?" Eddie asked simply. "Why now? What gives?"

"I don't know where this is going. If it hits the fan while I'm asleep, I want you to have a chance."

"What about you?" he asked.

"I have Dutch," Frank answered. "Go get some sleep," he suggested again. He turned to the dog and commanded "Dutch, come!"

Eddie watched the dog run up the stairs ahead of Frank to a room in a backwater Costa Rican hotel in a little known town. He wedged the gun in his belt, put on the sweatshirt, pulled it over the weapon and left the hotel for the plaza outside. He wanted fresh air and some time to think more than he wanted to sleep.

At forty thousand feet above the Caribbean Sea, a sleek, white Gulfstream jet streaked toward San Jose and was cleared for landing while still more than five hundred miles away. There would be no circling for this bird and no customs inspections for its passengers after it touched down. The pilots in the cockpit were in constant communication with the airport tower. Their runway was available as they approached. All air traffic was cleared from the skies for the Gulfstream. There was nary a hint in the radio chatter of why commercial air traffic patterns were disrupted for the jet.

The Gulfstream passed over the undeveloped beaches on the eastern coast and soared over the mountains to the Pacific side of Costa Rica. The plane made a wide loop over the west coast beaches and pointed its nose down toward the San Jose airport. Take-off from Washington, D.C. was just before dawn, and the sleek aircraft had flown ahead of the rising sun the entire trip.

"Welcome to Costa Rica, gentlemen," the pilot said over the intercom from the cockpit. "Touchdown in San Jose will be three minutes ahead of schedule thanks to a small tailwind," he added. Tom Aikens didn't care. Being on time was all that concerned him.

The team of men from the Gulfstream immediately boarded black, armor-plated SUVs waiting on the side of the runway with their engines running and the air conditioning turned up full blast. As the convoy of SUVs left the runway, the Gulfstream was towed to an empty hangar and encircled with a security perimeter, and preparations began for take-off on three minutes or less notice. The plane would remain in a state of readiness as long as Tom Aikens was on the ground in Costa Rica.

"To the embassy, sir?" a driver asked as Aikens took a swig from a bottle of cold water.

"No, Limon. Contact Captain Ruiz, the police commander. Get me some face time with him."

"Understood, sir," the driver said without any hesitation as he headed the vehicle toward the eastern shore. Two hours and one hundred miles later, Aikens was in Limon in the same office with the photographs on the wall where Frank had been interrogated.

Ruiz was annoyed. Aikens sensed his anger was mutable, however. The police captain understood law enforcement at all levels. More importantly, he understood politics. He wanted something, and Aikens understood he needed to leave something behind. The Washington intelligence chief scanned the wall of photographs. Ruiz might have future value, especially if any of these photographs represented more than simple grip-and-grin opportunities.

"I was asked to observe some people, help in a situation," Captain Ruiz said, "and then a woman ends up dead in my city. Her identity papers showed her to be Cheryl Norris, and photographs showed her to know an American living in this area named Frank Reardon. I was greatly embarrassed when *Senor* Reardon demonstrated the dead woman was not Cheryl Norris. Then your State Department demanded ... politely, but demanded nonetheless ... he be released," Ruiz continued. "Your people embarrassed me in front of your State Department. Now there is this dock fight, and he's taken off with one of Felix Mendoza's men. I am not a man who enjoys feeling foolish, *senor*."

"Captain, I stand before you an apologetic man. I take full responsibility for the actions of my people. I do not want you to feel any embarrassment. I will make it clear to all the appropriate people, including anyone you specifically wish to name, that this mix-up was not your fault and that you acted with only the highest personal integrity and professionalism," Aikens said. "Simply put, I am asking that you trust me to restore and enhance your reputation before my government. Captain, the United States values your friendship," the intelligence chief said, with his hands outstretched and palms facing up. In another country Aikens would simply push a briefcase full of cash across the desk and end the matter. That wasn't going to happen here. This cop already had wealth, connections, and something else, a deep sense of personal integrity.

The policeman stood at his desk, hands clasped behind his waist while Aikens sat in the same visitor's chair Frank had sat in when he was interrogated. In his mind the captain had accepted Aikens' apology. He'd wait before saying so, however.

"Captain, let's be honest with each other. You know the way of the world. I need to offer something here to accompany this apology. I don't wish to offend you. I know your station in this country. I also know you are trying to improve police methods and bring them to a higher level of professionalism," Aikens said.

The captain acknowledged Aikens.

"I can arrange for fifteen training slots at FBI headquarters for your department, men of your selection."

The captain smiled. "Thirty slots," he said, "and it is non-negotiable."

"Done," Aikens said, extending his right hand in friendship.

"Good, this unpleasantness is over. Now I suggest we exchange information on this murder, the Norris woman, *Senor* Reardon, and everything else," the cop said.

Aikens nodded in agreement, but he knew the flow of his information to the cop had to be timed carefully.

Over the next two hours Aikens listened to the captain's story of finding Frank, his description of the ex-cop's attitude, and how Frank didn't buckle under intimidation. What happened with the mission was becoming clear to Aikens. It seemed now the freelance FBI operative assigned to connect with the drug gang was killed, and his girlfriend came down here to complete the deal. Then Cheryl arrived in the country, only to be sucked deeply into the affair. Somehow the two must have been connected. Cheryl may have tried to interfere in the drug deal. And Reardon, a hard-nosed ex-cop and old friend from long ago, just happened to be in the same place at the wrong time. What a mess, Aikens thought.

"I'll want to talk with the Mendoza man Reardon lumped up," Aikens said.

"You're welcome to try, *senor*. He refuses to talk. I don't have much to hold him on, either. Officially, he's the victim of an assault," the captain said.

"Yes," Aikens sighed, "and with *Senor* Reardon on the loose not countering his statement, his story is all you have," Aikens finished for him.

The captain nodded.

Farther north at a Nicaraguan border crossing into Costa Rica, Martin Greco scrunched down in his seat at the back of a bus with a faded Boston Red Sox baseball cap pulled down over his unshaven face. He wore dirty jeans, a Nike sweatshirt and mud-encrusted construction boots. His coat was stained with a combination of sweat, oil and grime. He pretended to be asleep while a border guard, clutching an automatic weapon to his chest, casually strolled through the bus eyeballing the passengers. The guard had boarded the bus for a routine check of the migrant workers traveling to and from farm jobs along both sides of the border. Greco slowly opened one eye. From under the bill of his dirty old cap he alternately stared at the floor and watched the guard's movements.

During the next forty-eight hours, a team of highly trained mercenaries, handpicked by Greco and posing as sleeping migrant workers, would cross the border in other rickety old buses. The mercenaries would rendezvous with Greco at a camp set up on an out-of-the-way farm.

Each man, Greco included, crossed the border unarmed. Weapons for the team were waiting in Costa Rica. The team leader never moved armed men across borders unless they were on their way directly to a target. Transporting weapons was an unnecessary risk in Greco's business. Guns were simply tools, disposable and readily available anywhere. All it took was cash.

Not being Hispanic, Greco was the biggest risk at the border. So he opted to travel alone. His Mediterranean skin tone and unshaven look improved his chances of slipping into the country, as long as he didn't draw any unnecessary attention to himself.

The guard moved up and down the aisle of the old school bus again. He stopped and stared at Greco. The Washington man didn't flinch. He heard the guard's toe-tapping on the steel floor of the bus. He felt the guard's eyes scan him.

Greco never moved. Time stood still. In his mind he counted "one-Mississippi, two-Mississippi, three-Mississippi, four-Mississippi, five-Mississippi." Finally, he heard the boots of the border guard trudge to the front of the bus.

Greco remained frozen. At last, the guard stepped off the bus and ordered the driver to move out. The driver yanked on the mechanical arm to close the door and shifted his vehicle into gear. It lurched forward and proceeded down the road. None of the passengers moved or made sound until the bus traveled at least a mile. Chatter among the workers then started, and there was rampant speculation why they were detained.

Greco lifted the bill of his cap and just peered out the window.

Six

Frank trudged into the hotel room and dropped his duffle bag on the floor. Dutch stalked the perimeter of the room. The dog sniffed and poked his snout into every available nook and cranny before he quietly curled up in a corner. The room had one twin bed, a dresser with a cracked mirror, and two wooden chairs. The ceiling paint was yellowing and dried wallpaper was peeling away from the wall. An aging electric fan sputtered and spun from the ceiling above. Outside and down on the street, chickens clucked as they roamed about. There was no television or telephone in the room.

Frank dragged himself over to the door and wedged the back of a chair tightly under the doorknob and then flopped on the bed. He was asleep almost instantly, and then the nightmares started. Almost every night he was tortured by the recurring memories of being shot and visions of how Susan's life ended in their home that same night.

In his dream, Frank was sitting at a bar having a drink. Someone came rushing in and screamed a robbery was going down in the grocery next door. Frank sprinted out of the bar and rushed down the alley after the thief. Ahead of him in the alley, the man turned and fired a gun. Frank ducked behind a dumpster as the bullet ricocheted off the metal top and then bounced off the brick wall above his head. Small pieces of red brick rained down on the ground around him. The shooter turned a corner and disappeared. The dream always continued with Frank stepping out from behind the dumpster to give chase. Then the man, gun in hand, reappeared in the alley. Backlit, the thief leveled his weapon at Frank and in slow motion fired three times, hitting him in the chest. Every night Frank felt the three shots thump into his body.

In his nightmare he slumped to the ground, oozing blood and gasping for air. Over and over, the scene was always the same ... the chase, gunfire, bullets hitting him, and then slowly falling to the ground. And there was the laugh, the snickering sounds the man made as Frank rolled over on his side bleeding.

During the actual attack, Frank never saw the shooter's face. He simply remembered his laugh. The laugh was burned into his memory.

Sometimes in his dream the shooter had the face of a circus clown, big wide eyes, huge floppy ears, ruby red lips and wild hair, all atop a body dressed in a dark jacket and jeans. In his nightmare, the shooting always happened slowly.

Frank was also haunted by a nightmare of Susan's death. He knew his own suffering firsthand. He could only imagine Susan's suffering that night. Knowing the two shootings were connected made him feel responsible and angry.

He had been told about Susan in a cold, matter-of-fact police manner by his partner, Don Pruka. Straight up was the only way Don knew how to give Frank the news.

The shooter entered the house with a key taken from Frank's shot-up body. The cops believed the assailant surprised Susan in the kitchen of their house in

Bridgeport's middle class North End. A spilled pot of tomato sauce was found on the kitchen floor. The killer put two shots into Susan's heart at close range. She died instantly.

There were no reports of screams. Nothing was believed to have been stolen from the small, Cape Cod-style home. Other than the spilled pot on the floor near where the body was discovered, nothing in the home was disturbed. Nobody in the neighborhood heard the gunshots. Susan's body was discovered when the cops came to tell her Frank had been shot.

Pruka led the investigation and quietly kept copies of everything, official and otherwise, knowing Frank would want to see it all if he recovered. The police found the gun placed on the kitchen table. It had no fingerprints on it. Later the detectives determined the gun was stolen. It was part of a truckload of surplus military weapons stolen a year earlier during a hijacking about thirty miles west of a truck stop in the heartland of Iowa.

In his nightmare, Frank saw the killer standing over Susan smiling. It was the cold-hearted smile of a killer who enjoyed taking a life. And then there was the laugh, the snicker that haunted him.

When Frank was released from the hospital, and even before he returned to work, he started his own investigation. At first, the department and his friends tried to be understanding, but soon a contingent met with Pruka to get Frank to back off. Frank became insulting and critical of what had been done. He found fault with people who worked long hours, on and off duty, to find the shooter. Everyone was baffled, and the double shooting was fast becoming a cold case.

In a fit of anger, Frank decided to work the case alone. Tensions flared between Pruka and Frank as he followed leads without telling his partner. Alone, he retraced every step he took that night, from the bar stool he sat on when the robbery happened at the grocery next door to examining the dumpster hit by the first bullet. The department bosses called him in and suggested he might have come back to work too soon. The detective unit captain pressed him into counseling, something he tried with reluctance.

Frank wasn't satisfied just to read the reports from out-of-state cops. How a gun stolen from a truck in Iowa made its way to Bridgeport always puzzled Frank. He needed to speak to the truck driver. He took three vacation days and went to Dubuque to interview the truck driver firsthand. Frank found Big Bobby sitting on his porch having a beer after an overnight run.

"I just got back a little while ago," he said. "Did six hundred and seventy miles round trip from Dubuque to Omaha, fifteen hours including loading and unloading," Bobby said. "Get yourself a cold one." He pointed to a red-and-white cooler on the porch. The truck driver was right out of central casting, wearing faded blue jeans over ankle-high work boots and a blue-and-white flannel shirt with the sleeves ripped off. Underneath Frank saw a grey Chicago Bears T-shirt.

"I suppose you want to go over the hijacking again, huh?" Bobby asked.

"If you don't mind," Frank answered.

The truck driver went through his story again, as he had dozens of times before with local cops, federal investigators and military cops, all of them looking into the theft of the guns. Big Bobby said they searched his truck and his home on the chance he was involved. Each time his story was the same.

No connection was ever made between the truck driver and the theft of the guns. No one thought this simple, fly over-country truck driver was capable of masterminding a heist of this magnitude.

Frank went over every detail. He pulled out from his briefcase copies of reports from all the investigators and reviewed the most miniscule details with Bobby. The truck driver answered politely and consistently, as he had in past interviews. Frank persisted and became more strident. "So you just opened up the truck and gave up the weapons?"

"The guy had a gun on me!" Bobby answered.

"Yeah, you said that. Explain to me again, just like that you opened up the truck and gave him the guns?" Frank paused and leafed through a notebook. "How many weapons was that, now?"

"Mister, just what are you getting at?"

"Just trying to understand. You calmly gave up a load of weapons to a lone guy on the side of the road, and you have no witnesses to this story of yours," Frank pressed.

Bobby stood up. "Story? It ain't no damn story!" he said, raising his voice and struggling to retain control of himself. "Look, I got a wife, kids. I don't get paid to get killed."

"So," Frank pushed on, "let me get this straight. It was just you and this gunman. He forces you off the road and takes the weapons, and there were no witnesses? Right?" Frank summarized.

Bobby stood erect and clenched his fists. Frank smiled. He was starting to get a reaction from the truck driver.

"Now, listen. I've been nice to you 'cause I know who you are and that you lost your missus. I'm sorry for you and your loss, but I ain't taking any crap. I don't think that New England badge carries any weight around here. If you want to talk any more about the hijacking, you come back with cops from around these parts. We're done talking," Big Bobby said. "Get outta here."

Back in his highway motel room, Frank stretched out on the hard bed. He was just getting comfortable when there was pounding at the door. Frank opened it and found the town's chief of police and a patrolman standing in front of him.

Frank was told by the chief, one cop to another cop, to go back to Bridgeport. Big Bobby had complained. "You get some real reason to come back, call me. If we find something, we'll call you," the chief told him. "Right now, you have to go home. Tonight would be best. Pack and we'll drive you to the airport."

Back in Bridgeport, Frank walked into a dressing-down from his own chief of police. The Iowa cops had called Bridgeport. He was reprimanded for conducting an investigation off the books and, as the chief put it, "generally being a pain in the ass and causing trouble with another police department."

After Frank retired, Central America became his refuge. It was a place for him to try to forget his past and avoid people who felt sorry for him. His new home, however, offered no answers as to why things happened the way they did. The unresolved search for Susan's killer loomed over him as unfinished business. He knew in his heart that someday he'd have to return and resolve things. Someday.

Several hours after falling asleep in the San Sebastian hotel room, he woke up dripping in sweat from his nightmares. No matter the weather, the cold of New England or the blazing sun of Costa Rica, he always awoke from his unconscious torture dripping wet.

Today he woke with a case of the shakes, too. Frank gripped the sides of the mattress for a few minutes until his mind slowed down and he regained his sanity. He scanned the room without moving until he spotted Dutch sitting by the window, quietly surveying the street below. Stumbling over to the window, still dopey from exhaustion, Frank extended a shaky hand to stroke the dog's head.

"Good boy," he said, patting the dog. "We'll take care of each other," he said.

Frank looked to the dog for inspiration, and he was actually envious of the animal. Dutch's serenity was Frank's dream. First, he needed to get past the nightmares and the cold sweats on awakening. "You teach me, boy," he said to the dog. "You teach me what I need to learn."

Looking out the window of the hotel, Frank spotted Eddie sitting at a table of a café on the plaza. Stretched out in a chair with his legs crossed and one arm slung over the back, Eddie was drinking a beer. Frank shook his head, stumbled over to the door and kicked loose the old wooden chair he had shoved under the doorknob. Still half asleep, he made his way downstairs and across the street to Eddie.

"Hi ya, sleepy," Eddie said cheerfully as Frank approached. Eddie got a better look at Frank as he came closer. "Man, you look like crap."

"Sleep was more important to me than *cerveza*," Frank said as he sat down, eyeing Eddie's beer bottle. "It should have been more important to you, too," he lectured.

"That's one opinion," Eddie said. "It looks like you didn't get too much sleep anyway. You OK?" he asked.

Frank was staring again, this time at Eddie. He said nothing. Eddie knew the former cop was thinking, mulling something over in his head.

"I'll be fine," he said, running his fingers through his hair. When the waiter came over, Frank looked up at him and simply said, "Whiskey, *amigo*."

Eddie said nothing. Frank was a man who looked askance at someone drinking beer in the morning, only to order whiskey for himself. *This is a tormented soul*, Eddie thought.

"Ask," Eddie finally said.

"What?"

"Go ahead, ask me," he said. "Let's finish the interrogation you started at sea."

Frank finally said, "What's your story? You're more than a guy with a beer. How did you wind up down here?"

Eddie drained his beer and ordered another.

"I was a kicker," Eddie said.

"Explain," Frank replied.

"I've worked all over the world. Whenever Uncle Sam needed to supply some rebels or under-equipped government troops, sides didn't really matter very much. We would fly in aboard C-123 cargo planes at eight thousand feet, drop the rear hatch and kick out a load of supplies, medicine, food, electronics, but mostly weapons. I was a kicker, a guy in the belly of those flying tractor-trailers," Eddie said. "I dropped goods to so-called friends all over the world. Sometimes I'd do ground surveillance, a head count, or assess the fire in their bellies for a fight. One night on a low-altitude drop, a place you don't need to know, we got hit by a guy firing a shoulder-fired surface-to-air missile. We crashed into the jungle. The other three guys in the plane were killed. I was captured by the wrong people on the wrong side of the wrong hill. I was the perfect patsy. It was easy for the government to say I was a mercenary acting on my own."

Frank listened. He said nothing. He stared deeply into Eddie's eyes, right down to his soul. Finally, he said "Continue."

Eddie felt as if he were commanded to answer. "After I was grabbed up, a guy in D.C. that I dealt with had a sense of honor and pressed people to get me back," Eddie continued. "He went to the honchos in Washington and said they sent me in, and they damn well owed it to me to try and get me out. Two months later I was taken to the border and literally thrown over the line into the waiting arms of three guys in suits and sunglasses. They whisked me away, first to Washington and then to some Virginia horse farm, for a month of intensive debriefing."

"And then?" Frank asked.

"I was given a pension, only I got bored. I reconnected with some buddies, and they offered me a way to supplement my retirement under the table. I was sent down here to eyeball things. No flying, no guns, no nothing. And that's all I did until you showed up. Getting on your boat was more than I needed to do. I still don't know why I did it."

Frank mulled the story over in his head. He didn't judge anything.

"Why don't I just call them for help?" Eddie suggested.

"No," Frank answered emphatically.

"Why not?" Eddie shot back.

"I suspect we are looking at this mess from different angles."

"Come on," Eddie pleaded. "These guys are Americans, the good guys."

"Remember that girl on the slab in Limon?" Frank queried.

Eddie nodded.

"Well, she was an American, too, and now she's dead," Frank said.

"So what now?" Eddie asked. "Are we officially on a mission to find this woman from your past?"

"I asked you before if you were in or out. This time I need an answer," Frank said.

Eddie looked at him and nodded. "I'm in. We look for the woman."

"And we do it my way," Frank said. "I need to know now. No surprises."

"Your way," Eddie said, "we'll make a great team, a washed-up ops guy and a retired cop with a head full of nightmares, and both of us being chased by drug dealers.

Just tell me, where are we headed, and what are our chances?" Eddie asked.

Frank ignored Eddie's concerns. "We go up the coast. I know one of the guys the fat man mentioned. If we can get to him before Mendoza's people do, we might pick up a lead," Frank said.

With one gulp, Frank downed a shot of whiskey as the morning sun rose in the sky.

Seven

The two Americans and Dutch boarded an old bus that snaked through hamlet after hamlet, stopping to let people on and off at unmarked points along the pothole-filled dirt road. Every village was a haphazard collection of bars, hair braiding shops, *grocerias* and car repair shops.

Finally, Frank saw a broken fence surrounding a familiar taco restaurant in the distance. "We get off here," he prodded Eddie.

The two *gringos* stepped off the bus and immediately became objects of curiosity among the *peones*. Standing on the broken concrete slab of a sidewalk, the two men watched the bus drive away, spewing a cloud of foul-smelling diesel fuel into the air. This was not a tourist town. There were no excursions being offered from this town to nearby ancient Mestizo ruins or lush coffee plantations, and these two Americans were clearly outsiders.

Eddie looked around at the shacks and huts that made up the village and said nothing. The little town on the bus route was one hurricane away from being a swamp. It was a place familiar to him, a scar on the Central American countryside. There were places identical to this no-name hamlet all over the world, places he had been to in Asia and Africa. Eddie surreptitiously gathered information in these types of places. The same feeling of uneasiness always hung in the air, and in every one of these towns was a scammer, someone who always looked for a way to cheat and steal rather than do an honest day's work. That was the kind of man Frank and Eddie came to this village to find.

Eddie Pettigrew knew all about small towns. Born and raised in Tyrell Points, North Carolina, his home was a dirty little spot wedged between two peaks in the Blue Ridge Mountains of Appalachia, home for moonshiners and generations of endless poverty.

One day he saw his opportunity. A recruiter for the U.S. Army showed up in town and set up a small office in the post office. Eddie went to see him, lied about his age, and came back the next day with a backpack of personal things. He was ready to go wherever they wanted to send him.

Several months later he was shipped out to Vietnam, where he saw more small, broken-down villages and towns. They were just the start of a long string of such settlements yet to come in his life. In many ways Eddie was as broken down as this Costa Rican town. After his second hitch, he was recruited by the intelligence community to do its bidding.

Eddie wasn't like Frank. His new friend was a guy on a personal mission, he cared about people. He cared about this woman, someone he hadn't seen in years. And once again, Eddie found himself helping someone else with his agenda.

In the village Frank was searching for a small-time thug who would have made it his business to have information about Cheryl Norris. Across the road Frank eyed a small restaurant with a plank of wood over the entrance with the name Hector's hand-painted on it.

"There," Frank said, pointing to the restaurant.

Eddie didn't say anything. Crossing the rutted street slowly, he swept his head back and forth and took in their surroundings. He noted every shack and parked car and made mental notes on every guy hanging out under a tree or in a doorway.

The restaurant was more of a bunker than a building. It was constructed in the typical hurricane-defense style of the region, four cinder block walls that stood about five-feet high. On each corner of the rectangular cement box was a pole. Inside, right in the center of the eating area, surrounded by tables, was a fifth pole. All five poles supported one huge tent roof.

Immediately to the right of the entrance to the restaurant was an old door laid across the tops of two barrels that served as the bar. A handful of mismatched glasses were scattered on top of it. A few wobbly stools stood at the tabletop. Along the top of the wall behind the bar were bottles of cheap whiskey. A back corner of the bunker was partitioned off for use as the kitchen, where a woman stood stirring the pots. A potent mix of food smells filled the tented restaurant.

The two Americans took seats at a table in the corner that offered a view of the street and the back door. Both men made a silent surveillance of their surroundings. Patrons were only a few working people. Two young boys waited tables. In the corner, near the makeshift bar and cash register, a man stared warily back at them. Eddie sat silently while Frank ordered some food and told one boy to get his father. The boy's father heard the conversation and brought food. He immediately told the boy to leave.

"*Si, senor?*" he asked.

"*Donde esta Rafael, senor?*" Frank asked.

"Rafael? I know no such man, *senor.*" he said.

The switch to English made the negotiations easier. The owner was no longer able to feign ignorance of English and an inability to communicate with Frank.

"You know who I want, where do I find him? This doesn't have to be difficult. Once we speak with him, we'll leave."

The two boys had disappeared. In the kitchen, pots were still bubbling away on the stove, and the woman was gone too.

"He's here, isn't he, *senor?*' Frank asked.

Quietly, a man who had slipped into the restaurant after Frank and Eddie approached their table.

"Reardon, we meet again. Who is your companion?" a thin man with a moustache asked.

"Go," Frank ordered the restaurant owner. "Go to your family."

Rafael sat down, nodded at the man, and he scampered away. Rafael anticipated a unique opportunity for profit looming ahead. He hoped to conduct a private sale of information his bosses need not know anything about when he delivered the protection money he collected for them.

Frank eyeballed Rafael.

"I am looking for a woman."

Rafael grinned. Twirling a lit *cigarillo* and flashing a toothy grin, he pushed back off his forehead a short brimmed fedora hat that conjured up memories of the

Sinatra Rat Pack. Rafael's iteration of the style included three wooden matches with the red and white phosphorous tips wedged into the hat band. The matches stood straight up, like the martinis old Blue Eyes drank. He reached up and pinched the peak of the hat, and gently lifted it off his head, and casually dropped it on the table.

His hair was black as coal, slicked back across the top and sides of his head and tied tight in a little *coleta* matador knot. The squared-off bottom of his *Guayabera* shirt, with hand-stitched bright green and yellow patterns running down the front, hid his thumbs hitched on the waistband of his neatly creased trousers. His black leather shoes were perfectly laced and reflected a high gloss shine.

Both Americans turned their heads simultaneously as a whiff of his cheap cologne, mixed with the pungent smells of the peasant cooking in the kitchen, shot up their nostrils.

"Ah, a mission of love, you look for a *mujer*," Rafael said, waving his hand in the air in a grand gesture. "*Muy romantica.*"

Frank sighed. Rafael's attempt at humor was annoying.

"She's an American. She'll be on the run. I heard she was headed this way and I thought you might know something," Frank said.

"An American up here? Not many female tourists get this deep into the beauty of Costa Rica alone, *senor*," he said.

Frank wondered how much this game of cat and mouse was going to cost him.

Eddie decided to end the negotiations. He lurched over the table and with his two hands grabbed Rafael by the lapels of his embroidered shirt, yanked him forward, and slammed his face on the tabletop. For good measure, Eddie lifted Rafael's head and bounced it on the wood table a second time.

"Look, you little asshole. We're here looking for someone. Tell us what you know, and we'll leave a few bucks on the table. Jerk us around for another minute and I'll start busting you up. Get my drift, *senor*?" Eddie said.

Bent over the table, the village thug sputtered and trembled.

"I know people. You're going to be sorry, *senor*!"

"Well, they'd better be coming through that door in the next thirty seconds to do you any good, *amigo*."

Eddie glared into his victim's eyes. Rafael shot a look over to Frank.

"Don't look at him, look at me!" Eddie commanded.

Frank slid his chair back, folded his arms and shrugged. "Rafael," Frank said softly, "*mi amigo* seems upset."

Then Rafael surrendered.

"*Si, si, senor*. I may know something. But I expect to be paid," Rafael said, making a futile last attempt to retain some modicum of control over the situation.

Eddie lifted him off the table and slammed him down again, harder, so his head bounced off the edge, giving him an immediate bruise. "Don't piss me off, just talk, or I'll make you eat the money!"

Rubbing the side of his head and looking at Eddie warily, he said, "OK, OK, but you're not going to believe it. It's a *loco* story. *Muy loco*," Rafael said, still rubbing his head.

Rafael spent the next hour telling Frank and Eddie about a farm in a valley beyond the mountains run by a disenfranchised Mennonite minister who broke away from the main congregation in neighboring Belize. In Belize the Mennonites had huge land holdings and had become a major component of the country's agricultural economy. In exchange for their contributions to the country's well-being, they were left alone by the government to practice their religion unencumbered by bureaucratic entanglements. This was the first time either Frank or Eddie heard of a Mennonite encampment in Costa Rica, or anywhere this far south in Central America.

Rafael told them of a man who called himself Father Blanco. He operated a farm in a valley protected by the hills as a refuge for women who ran away from abusive husbands around the world. Underground networks throughout North America and elsewhere helped battered women escape to Father Blanco's farm to reclaim a sense of calmness in their life. Later, they left with new identities and a new life.

"If she is here, she is with Father Blanco. It would be the only safe place for a *gringo* woman here alone," Rafael said. "Sometimes a few women come to the town with Father Blanco or his men to get supplies, but they rarely speak to anyone. He frowns on it."

"What stops the crazy husbands from showing up down here to reclaim their wives?" Frank asked.

"Mendoza does," Rafael said.

Frank and Eddie exchanged glances. "Explain," Frank said.

"Father Blanco wants total privacy. He allows no one on the farm, no *policia*, no visitors, absolutely nobody. Nobody except Mendoza; he is allowed access to a small air strip. In exchange for this right of way on Father

Blanco's farm, Mendoza guarantees the security of the entire property and the safety of the women," Rafael said.

"And these identities," Eddie said, "how do they get created? How does a priest or minister or whatever Father Blanco is create new identities for women from around the world?"

"That too is done through Mendoza," he said.

"A *jefe cocainero* is guaranteeing the virtue of women?" Eddie queried.

"*Si, senor.* He doesn't tolerate any trouble at the farm or toward the women. Even with his own men he is very strict. It's a price he gladly pays for a private landing field for his planes traveling from Colombia through Central America to *los Estado Unidos*," Rafael said. "It is said he limits the field to emergency uses."

The *gringos* looked at each other. Both Americans knew Central America had become the primary corridor for drug runners as American interdiction programs heated up in the Caribbean islands.

"I heard him in the *cantina* once telling Father Blanco his farm was his insurance policy," Rafael continued.

"Really?" Eddie said, keeping the conversation alive.

"A few months ago," Rafael said, "three of Mendoza's men started teasing some of the women who came to town for supplies. It was silly stuff, poking at them, asking them to run away with them. Whispers washed through the village that Mendoza was angry at the men, and they disappeared. Then a week later, over the course of three days, one was found each morning at sunrise, chained to the fountain in the square, severely beaten, with a note tied to his ankle saying he was punished for insulting the women.

The Americans said nothing.

"*Es verdad*," Rafael continued.

"This has a stink to it," Frank said.

"*Es verdad*," Rafael repeated, fearing another head-banging from Eddie.

"There's more to this farm than vegetables and Father Blanco's charity work," Frank said.

"Yep, probably so," Eddie replied. "It's also probable your lady friend has sought refuge with Father Blanco not knowing the truth about him. And that, my friend, may have been a dangerous decision for her. If Blanco and Mendoza are in cahoots, she's run right into the arms of the bad guys at full speed," Eddie said.

"We need to get to that farm," Frank said. "We need to see Father Blanco."

"Not possible," Rafael shot back.

"We'll need to recon the farm's perimeter," Eddie said. "How do we get there, Rafael?"

"No, you can't go up to the farm," Rafael said. "I won't tell you where it is!" he said, pushing back from the table to avoid another assault from Eddie.

"You know that as soon as we leave here this guy is going to sell us out to Mendoza," Eddie told Frank bluntly.

"Not if we take him along as our guide to Father Blanco's farm," the former cop said, staring at his food.

"You're planning on taking this character to the jungle? He doesn't strike me as the outdoors type. And you're going to trust him, too? Isn't this the guy you talked about back on the boat who talks to Mendoza? We're going to trust this guy?"

"Well, you already pointed out we can't leave him here," Frank said.

"Wait!" Rafael protested. "I am not going with you. I just told you I won't even tell you where Father Blanco's farm is located. Not me, I won't go!" he wailed.

Frank leaned in and said quietly, "Rafael, half this town already knows we're talking to you. By tonight everyone will know we spoke to you. If we go into the jungle and tramp around on our own, we're bound to find the farm. And when we do, people will assume it was because you told us. So save us some trouble. Mendoza already knows we're in the area. How long will it be until he hears we spoke to you? He won't think I looked you up just for old time's sake," the former cop said.

Frank looked over his shoulder and saw Hector standing with his wife, clutching his children in the kitchen. "Think for a second, who does that old man in the back fear more, you or Mendoza? He'll talk to save his kids, not your skinny ass. Just come with us like a good boy."

Eddie rolled his eyes and looked over at his new partner. "We'll need weapons."

Without looking up from his food Frank said, "Rafael, see to that for me, OK?"

Rafael just stared at him. Frank looked at him and repeated, "See to that now!" The skinny man left in a hurry as Hector and his family watched in fear from the kitchen area.

"It sounds like Mendoza is using this farm as a back-up facility when things get hot up in Nicaragua and Honduras, Frank said. "Mendoza is a businessman. In his line of work, he also needs a quiet place to set down a plane and hide out if he learns of trouble waiting for him up ahead. Father Blanco's field is probably his safe house."

"What's with the deep concern about the women?" Eddie asked. "It would seem they would be the sweets of a candy store for him and his men. Why is he so concerned about their well-being?" Eddie questioned.

"I don't know, maybe he's just avoiding trouble. Somehow that doesn't seem likely. There's more to that angle of the operation. We'll figure it out," said Frank, still the cop.

"So, what's the plan? We go into the hills, find the farm, and then what?" Eddie asked.

"Maybe we make it uncomfortable for him to do business around here."

"And the women?"

"I haven't figured that out yet," Frank said. "They are women who would be difficult to trace to him, and he sets them up with new identities. Mendoza has some use for that sort of human capital."

"You think he's using them as mules for his dope?" Eddie queried.

"Not likely, the volume they might be able to transport across the border is too small. He's too big a player in the drug business to be so concerned about the investment he's making in these women. He needs them for something more important than being a mule."

Eddie agreed.

"I'm going to check on Rafael," Eddie said as he left the restaurant.

Alone, Frank's thoughts drifted back to the summer at Hammonasset Beach. It was a summer when all he and his friends cared about was the sunshine. Life was simpler. Life was about the water, cold beers and cookouts.

From underneath Frank's chair, Dutch suddenly let loose with a low growl. "Easy, boy," Frank said softly as he dropped his hand to scratch the dog behind his ear. "I know he's there. Easy does it."

Tom Aiken's driver took him to a cliff over Limon so he could call Greco undisturbed on his satellite telephone. Greco and his team had crossed the border and reached their camp undetected. On the phone Aikens and Greco updated each other on the status of the mission. The Washington chief filled in his Number One about his conversation with the police captain.

"It seems like Reardon is on a rescue mission for this Norris woman. The drug lord Mendoza is probably after Reardon, as well, believing the Norris woman has the disc or knows where it is. We're still chasing our tail on this case. I don't like that," Aikens complained.

"I agree. We need to get out in front of this," Greco said. "I found a guy Reardon roughed up and dumped in the water. He's a Mendoza man." Greco told Aikens the story about the fat man and the shark. "It's the kind of thing that will become legend down here in a short time. Once Mendoza hears of it, he'll have to top the legend."

"Or destroy it," Aikens cut in. "It's a machismo thing, and it happened in Mendoza's own backyard. He can't let it go unchecked, not something like this done by an outsider."

"For the moment all I see us being able to do is locate Reardon and stake him out as a lamb for the wolf," Greco said. "Mendoza doesn't know we're here. All he knows is

Reardon is dinging around in his backyard. He can't be happy about that. We just follow the bread crumbs until they lead us somewhere."

"That's a dangerous plan," Aikens said. "That kind of approach has lost two people in this mission already."

"I know," Greco said, "but others made that mess, not my team. I didn't put Reardon or anyone else into the field," he said, referring to the FBI team that originally concocted the plan.

"I hate mopping up for someone else's mistakes," Aikens said.

Eight

Frank stepped out of Hector's cement box restaurant for a cigarette. He flicked a small butane cigarette lighter and without lifting his head, he lit a cigarette and tilted his eyes upward to peer over his fingertips. Lurking in the alley between Hector's and the business next door he spied a man in camouflage pants and jump boots. He wore a black T-shirt that stretched tightly across a chest sculpted by many hours of physical training.

Frank slipped his lighter back into his pants pocket, took a drag off the cigarette, and casually strolled back into Hector's *taqueria*. Once inside and in the shadows, he dropped to a crouch and moved slowly along the inside of the cinder block wall. He looked at Hector and commanded him to be silent, putting his forefinger to his lips. Quietly, he maneuvered along the wall to the rear of the restaurant. He rose silently and slipped into the kitchen area. Over the cinder blocks he watched the man in the camouflage pants cautiously edge his way toward the street.

Frank tiptoed out the back door of the restaurant and crouched down again against the rear wall. He poked his head around the corner of the wall and saw the man jerking his head left and right, trying to locate Frank on the street. Frank pulled his head back as the stranger hurriedly went back down the alley.

As the man approached the back corner of the restaurant, Frank jumped up and drove a left-handed punch into the man's stomach that doubled him over. He came down on the stranger's face with a powerful right punch, knocking him down to one knee. The man struggled to get up. Frank quickly dropped an empty metal garbage can over his head, grabbed its handle and ran the man into the cinder block wall. Frank bounced his victim off the back wall of the restaurant several times. The man's head pinged inside the can as if it were a single bean trapped in a maraca. In defeat, the man dropped to the ground unconscious.

Seeing the assault, Eddie rushed down the alley and helped Frank move the unconscious man to a remote area behind the restaurant.

"Christ, you never go after a guy halfway, do you?"

"He's younger and stronger. I don't count on getting second chances. Check that Jeep," Frank said, pointing to a vehicle hidden in the brush. "I think it's his."

"Who is this man?" Rafael squealed as he approached the fight scene. "Is he with Mendoza?"

"Mendoza may be a hardass about his guys messing around with Father Blanco's women, but he equips them pretty good," Eddie said, examining an Italian-made assault weapon that he pulled from the Jeep. He clicked the safety on and off and aimed the gun down the alley at an imaginary target. "Sweet, real sweet," he said.

"This isn't a Mendoza man," Frank said, looking down at his victim. "Check this out, you've worked with spooks before. Tell me how all this adds up. That plaything in your hand comes from Italy, his clothes are Australian commando issue, and he's wearing Czech boots. And this knife is British. Do you think some drug runner's paid muscle would be that much of a world shopper?"

Frank stretched out his victim's arm. "Look here, a tattoo has been removed from his arm. Why would Mendoza care about some old body ink?"

"He's a mercenary," Eddie said quietly and confidently. "He's sanitized. Nothing on him or about him is traceable." The one-time CIA kicker knew the drill. "This guy probably hasn't even used a bar of soap in the past month from the country that employs him," Eddie said. "He's one of ours."

"What do you mean? He's from America? He looks Hispanic. Explain," Rafael demanded.

"Actually, he's one of yours. This guy is with the people you work for," Frank said to Eddie with a tone of accusation in his voice.

"Wait just a minute!" Eddie protested. "I've been straight with you. No contact, that's what you wanted, no contact with the people I've worked for in the past. Don't blame me if those people act on their own."

"Who is he? Who does he work for?" Frank asked.

"Him? Who is he personally? He's a face in the crowd, a hired gun. He's a better trained version of the guy you wanted to toss off your boat to the sharks," Eddie said.

"Sharks? *Madre Dios*," Rafael said, as the two *gringos* started to argue.

"Shut up," Frank said to Rafael. "Your pal Mendoza is no altar boy."

Rafael froze where he stood.

"That's right, I know you pass Mendoza information. Did you think I showed up here looking for you by accident? Just relax. We'll get to you later," Frank said to Rafael.

"So who does he work for?" Frank repeated, turning to Eddie.

"Send him on an errand," Eddie said, pointing to Rafael.

"Take a walk, Rafael, but not too far. We're pulling out soon, and you don't have too many options with Mendoza coming through here pretty soon."

The local snitch slid away. He knew Frank was right. His survival depended on the two Americans.

"OK, I do the eyes and ears thing for a guy in D.C. who runs a very high-end security operation," Eddie began. "My guy answers only to the President. He's the guy who got me out of that jam I told you about. It's a good bet this merc was hired by a team my guy put down here to take control of the operation you stumbled into. This drug thing your friend is involved with began as a sting. They staked out some guy in the U.S. as bait for a big fish down here. I think that fish is Felix Mendoza. I was just told to eyeball Mendoza's guys. My friend was peeved about this operation. He inherited it from some other agency when the wheels started to come off. When the cops dragged you in and you got yourself out, somehow that caught their attention. They wanted to know about your movements," Eddie said. "I haven't talked to anyone since we left Limon. That was my promise to you, to do this your way, and I've kept my word."

The two men continued talking as they examined the Jeep and its contents. Frank believed Eddie, and he was growing more comfortable with him. He found a handheld field radio and flipped it on. It crackled to life.

"Whatever friend you called to get sprung woke them up in D.C.," Eddie said. "As an aside to the operation down here, they want to know your friend's name."

"That's just D.C. paranoia. It's not relevant to anything happening here. They just can't stand some Connecticut flatfoot upstaging them," Frank laughed.

"You still want to keep them out of this? They might be helpful," Eddie observed.

"Nothing has changed. It seems all they've done so far is create a trail of dead bodies. I don't plan on joining that group. There may be a time they'll have something I need," Frank said. As he finished his sentence the radio in his hand came to life with a voice.

"Quintana, come in. Report, now."

"Do you know that voice?" Frank asked.

"No," Eddie said.

Frank clicked the transmitter button a few times and shut the radio off. "I found a bunch of stuff in the Jeep I want to take with us. It's piled on the front seat." He took a roll of cash from his pocket and peeled off five tens. "Give this to Hector; tell him we're sorry for upsetting his family. Then tie up our pal Quintana over here."

Frank picked up the British commando knife and slashed the tires of the Jeep and the spare that was bolted above the back bumper. He raised the hood and randomly ripped out wires and drove the blade into the radiator. He quickly slipped in the back door of the restaurant to the kitchen and grabbed a small box of sugar. With great care he poured two cups worth into the gas tank of the Jeep and screwed the gas cap back on the vehicle.

"Get Rafael, we're out of here," Frank said.

The two men gathered up the supplies from the Jeep and left the alley to get into a small truck Rafael had waiting on the curb.

"Drive." Frank said. "Just head up into the hills until I tell you to stop," he commanded.

Rafael didn't question the Americans. Frank stared at the transmitter they took from the Jeep and pondered his next move as they drove away.

"Where'd you get this truck?" Eddie asked Rafael.

"Drug runners abandon stuff all over the country," he answered calmly. "I take their leavings for use later. People around here have needs."

"And those needs get supplied for a price, I'll bet," Eddie remarked. Rafael said nothing in response.

"And the weapons?" Frank asked quietly, without looking at anyone.

"Same thing," Rafael said. "Things get left behind."

Frank eyed Eddie inspecting a rifle in the rear seat, slowly sliding his hands across the weapon.

"Do you miss that work? How long has it been since you used one of those things?"

"Huh, what do you mean? What are you talking about?" Eddie asked quickly.

"That rifle, it's a sniper rifle. That's what you did in the Army. You were a sniper, right?" Frank asked.

Eddie's jaw dropped. He never mentioned that part of his background to anyone in Costa Rica. It was a part of his life he hoped to leave behind. As the truck bounced down the road toward the hills, Eddie sat slack-jawed, starring at Frank. Finally, in a soft voice, he said, "This is a Czech weapon. It's not a bad piece of equipment, but it doesn't hold up in the field over the long haul. It's what you might call a disposable rifle. I used a customized M-14 model."

"How did you know I was a sniper?" Eddie asked after several minutes of silence.

Frank saw the subject was painful for his new friend. It was written across his face.

"I was a homicide cop. People and their body language were my business. You cuddle that rifle like a baby. You appreciate every contour of that weapon. Only someone who understood its use would react that way," Frank said with empathy.

Eddie stiffened and regained his composure. "OK, let's get something straight. I'm out of the game. I won't take someone out that way again. If we have to, I'll fight, but no sniper work," he declared.

"Hard to say what's ahead," Frank remarked casually.

"No sniper work; it's just that simple," Eddie said. "Deal with it."

The one-time sniper rubbed his thumb over a spot on the butt of the rifle, cleaning away some grime. Eddie took a tiny pocketknife out his pants and carefully scratched the letter T on the gun butt.

"What's that letter for?" Frank asked.

"Tyrell Points, my hometown," the ex-shooter said. "I mark all my weapons this way. It's my weapon now, and damn the person who says otherwise."

Frank didn't pursue the discussion. Eddie was a man with a tortured past, too. They had that in common, and it drew them together.

While Frank was sizing up Eddie for a fight yet to come, the sniper's mind spiraled back in time to his days in the U.S. Army and his evolution as a hotshot shooter.

Eddie's career as an Army sharpshooter-turned-sniper blossomed with the CIA. He was issued three M-14NM rifles with wood stocks custom-fitted to the curve of his shoulder and the length of his arm. He spent weeks sanding the stocks and carefully carving the initial T, for Tyrell Points, in script on the butts. He then shellacked, sanded, and re-shellacked the butts again to keep out any possible infusion of water from the humid climate in the jungles where he worked. The weapons, perfectly initialed, became an extension of him.

One day he was assigned to take down a North Vietnamese officer in a Cambodian village. The enemy was using the village as a camp while anti-aircraft batteries were being constructed across the border in Vietnam. Every time the American troops came to engage the enemy and attack the new gun emplacements, the Vietnamese soldiers scurried to safety across a shallow river into Cambodia.

His target took up residence in a hut with the young wife of a rice farmer. Eddie watched the officer drive the husband and children away. The officer kept the woman there with him. Through his scope Eddie saw the husband try to take his wife with him, only to get a rifle butt driven into his kidneys. Dejected, the man was forced to surrender and leave the village to protect his children.

The smart way was to take this guy down and free the woman with a single shot. Eddie planned to do it in broad daylight, with a smile, in front of all the officer's troops and the whole village. He was going to enjoy this kill.

Eddie learned every routine of the village over the next week. The commander unwound every day at the same time with a smoke. That was to be kill time, just as the Asian lit his cigarette.

The next day, he observed the officer coming back to the hut. The man disappeared into the hut and right on schedule reappeared and withdrew his cigarette. Eddie lined up his sight. He took a breath and held it. He watched the man cup the lit match with his hands to light his cigarette. The officer tossed the match away and drew in a long drag.

Eddie had his head dead center in his sights and fired. Just as he pulled the trigger, the officer bent over to flick something off his pants. The conical-shaped cartridge whizzed right over him and through the straw wall of the hooch behind him. A scream was heard almost instantly. The officer rushed in and immediately raced out again following a hysterical woman carrying a baby with a bloody head.

Eddie's bullet had missed the soldier and mortally wounded an infant inside the hut. He froze. Where the hell did that kid come from? He never saw the baby in the village. He gathered up his equipment and ran from his shooting perch. While racing through the jungle Eddie radioed for a chopper extraction. He made it to a clearing as the helicopter was touching down. He threw himself into the bird and balled himself up into a corner while a crewman ordered an immediate liftoff. Eddie said nothing to his rescuers on the flight back. When he returned to the base, Eddie told his CIA handlers he was through. He refused to take any more sniper missions.

The CIA tried to dissuade him. Some of his superiors threatened repercussions, possibly a court-martial.

"Do what you have to do," he said steadfastly. His mind was made up.

Finally, one of the bosses simply said, "Cut him loose. Just discharge him." Eddie drifted, first through Asia and then through South America. A year later, he was approached by the CIA again and offered the chance to be a kicker. With few other employment opportunities, he accepted. He was a government employee again.

The truck rolled through the countryside. Finally, Frank looked up from the radio he carried and eyed the road ahead. He saw where it started to lead into the hills.

"Go up that way, Rafael. Find an overlook of Father Blanco's farm and his airstrip," Frank said, pointing with the barrel of his pistol.

Rafael pulled the truck off the road and into the brush. "From here we walk, about a half mile."

Frank and Eddie, led by Rafael, crawled out onto a ledge on their stomachs. Eddie had the sniper rifle strapped to his back and a cloth tied around the opening of the barrel to keep the insides clean. Rafael quietly pointed down to fields below where about a dozen people were tending neatly laid out rows of crops.

"Father Blanco's farm," he said softly.

Surrounded by the Costa Rican jungle, the self-ordained minister and his band of followers had carved out a neatly working agricultural oasis in a small valley, far from the peering eyes of any authorities. Frank scanned the scene and observed about a half dozen armed men strolling around the edges of the fields and around the main house. The fields, the compound and the airstrip were all carved out of a valley in the jungle. A single road meandered through the dense overgrowth to Father Blanco's hideaway.

"This guy Blanco spent a lot of effort to build this. Look at the excess clearance around the fields, compound and airstrip. I think he's planning to expand," Frank said.

"It's a killing zone," Eddie said.

"What?"

"It's a clear area for him to repel attackers from the jungle. He doesn't want anyone to pop out of the trees and be on top of him. An attacking force would have to traverse the open area first," Eddie said, with the expertise of a military commander.

Frank stared at Eddie and understood the lesson.

"Who are his followers, and who are the women passing through?" Eddie asked.

No one answered. Frank was preoccupied trying to see if he could recognize any one of the women in the field as Cheryl. It had been years since he last saw her.

"You need a plan, my friend. This isn't some place where you can bust open a door and scream 'hands up, you're under arrest,'" Eddie advised. "You know in your heart, this place is really a Mendoza operation. I don't care what they call that guy down there, Father Blanco, Brother Blanco, he's a Mendoza guy working some kind of Mendoza operation. This is more than a street crime operation, my friend."

Frank looked at him and nodded. "You're right," he said.

Rafael exhaled. He fantasized the Americans would now simply go away. He glanced over at Frank and Eddie. They were intently studying the geography below them. He knew that both of them were silently measuring distances between points on the edge of the crop fields and the buildings. No, it was clear to him now, he saw it in their eyes. They were staying.

Nine

Back at Hector's, Greco and Aikens assessed the new damage to their mission and helped the man they had sent to track Frank and Eddie's movements, who was beaten up and left unconscious. Reardon's reaction to the surveillance made it clear to them he wanted to work solo. Greco feared there was little chance of ever gaining his cooperation. The rest of Greco's team fanned out through the village trying to gather intel on where the two Americans might be headed.

"We can fix the equipment issue," Greco said. "It's mostly childish vandalism," he added.

"Really? Do you think so? Did you see this?" Aikens asked, pointing to a line of sugar stuck around the rim of the gas cap of the disabled Jeep.

Greco looked puzzled.

"You've been in the jungle too long, my friend. This is an old city trick, one that is very effective."

Greco looked at him perplexed.

"You put sugar in a gas tank," Aikens said. "In a relatively short period of time, the fuel pump sucks it into the fuel system and then into the engine. The sugar combines with the gasoline mixture, and it becomes a goop. It works its way into the piston chambers. After a while, the whole engine seizes up and shuts down. It's bad enough when your engine craps out on the street. For you, however, a jungle fighter," Aikens said pausing, "it would be disastrous. I figure you'd be stranded about fifty miles from here, in the middle of some very hard country."

Greco made a low growl.

"I told you that this guy was good. Truth is, you might actually like him," Aikens said.

Greco, now short a vehicle and having further armed Frank with the weapons he confiscated, just grunted

"Focus on the mission, Marty," Aikens said. "Don't start branding Reardon an enemy just yet. He wants, at the very least, some of the same things we do."

"I suppose," Greco said, trying to exercise control over himself. "I noticed he took a field radio. We've been trying to raise a connection. There has been no response as of yet."

"That's good," Aikens said.

"How so?"

"If he took the radio, the possibility of communication hasn't been shut off. He's assessing us, trying to determine if we have any value to him and his goals. If he had already decided against that possibility, he never would have taken the radio," Aikens said. "Keep trying to raise him but with no pressure. Just aim to keep the door open," Aikens advised.

"OK, boss," Greco answered.

At the farm, Father Blanco stood on the porch of the main lodge building at the farm and scanned his domain. He ran his agricultural operation with the help of fundamentalist disciples who followed him to Costa Rica and a flow of battered women from around the globe who flocked to him for refuge. The mainstream Mennonite Church immediately disavowed him when he left Belize.

However, Father Blanco persevered and quickly established his new religious order, complete with a following, and tapped into a well-entrenched, secret underground that brought the battered women to him.

Each link in the chain led the women to the farm. A house here, a church there, no one host along the way knew more than the link behind them or ahead of them. And, as an added security precaution, changes in the links were frequent and without warning.

At the end of the chain, the women spent time working in the fields. Father Blanco determined when they were capable of leaving and re-entering the world. He bestowed upon the women new identities and established them in new lives, sometimes in the United States and sometimes in other countries. Their sisters on the farm never knew where they went. The women left behind simply wished the departing friends good luck and bade them farewell. Then the process began all over again.

Today he was very interested in an American woman. She was a new addition to his farm who found her way to his little piece of paradise without the help of the network. She passed herself unannounced from link to link and somehow made it to Costa Rica. Once there, she simply asked directions in town to the front gate of his farm.

Father Blanco was amazed. She had the resourcefulness to follow the chain without raising any suspicions among the hosts along the way, who normally would have alerted him. Her success also troubled him. It demonstrated a serious breakdown in security. The best course of action was to take her in and confine her until he had answers.

Father Blanco greeted Cheryl in the study of the main house, a huge room with an oak desk surrounded by four leather chairs. The minister's desk looked out over the four chairs to two opposing couches with a teak coffee table strategically placed between them. The table had a display of wooden animal figures carved by local Indians. There were floor to ceiling bookcases built into the walls, and between them were intricate tapestries depicting religious scenes.

"Calm yourself, my dear. Tell me what brings you to me," Father Blanco said, as he pointed her toward one of the leather chairs.

"I came to help a friend, but I fear she has been killed by drug runners. Now I think they are after me," she sobbed. "They think I have something of theirs. I need refuge. This is the only place I know in Costa Rica where I feel I can be safe."

Father Blanco looked at her cautiously. "Tell me exactly, how did you find this place? How do you know about the chain that leads here?"

Cheryl appeared agitated. She kept looking around and appeared to have trouble focusing on the conversation. "Oh, I work with a group in Minnesota that sends troubled women here. I know all about the underground. I've put women through it before," she said, whipping her head all around, looking at nothing in particular. Her fidgeting and lack of concentration was distracting to the minister. He wanted to grab her by the shoulders and tell her simply to sit. He wanted to chastise her as if she were a child. He restrained himself. Those attributes would not be seen as characteristic of a man of the cloth.

"Slowly, my child. You say your friend is involved in drugs?" he asked.

"Well, yes, I mean no, well, sort of. You see, her boyfriend was. Anyway, it's a long story," she babbled.

"I cannot countenance illegal activities or criminals," he said defensively.

"Yes, I understand, but it's not me. I was only trying to help my friend. Now I think she's dead," Cheryl rambled.

Father Blanco's head was spinning from Cheryl's rapid-fire speech.

"Please, slow down. We'll talk about your friend in a moment. Tell me how you managed to get here, and please tell me slowly," he implored.

"Oh, that. Like I said, I work with a woman's group in the Midwest. I've put women here before," she said.

"Into the underground, you placed women into the underground. How did you get all the way here through the underground. It's a very secure network," he said, not realizing he was projecting the sin of pride.

"Well, you don't think I'd put a woman in need into a dark underground and not know what was on the other end, do you? I researched the trail. I have documented contacts, safe houses, the whole bit," she explained.

"I've never heard of you," he said.

"So? Why would you? I never contacted you. I knew what I wanted, and that was enough. It was the safety valve for my women. I know where you put them and where they are today. I stay in contact with them and check their progress. Some use me to see their kids back home," Cheryl said.

This is not good, Blanco thought.

"And why did you utilize the underground to find your friend down here? Why didn't you simply come to Costa Rica and search for her?" Father Blanco asked.

"I couldn't do that because I knew my friend had gotten involved with drug dealers. I thought the best way to reach out to her was to keep a low profile. I knew she was in a desperate situation when I learned she had stolen all my identification papers and passport. Using the underground network, I was able to slip into Costa Rica quietly and set about trying to help her.

Father Blanco stood still and listened in disbelief. He wondered what to do with her. She made just enough sense to concern him, but it was not enough to explain everything fully.

"Just what is it you have that these men want from you?" Father Blanco asked slowly. He rubbed his temples, trying to assess everything and still gather more information from the new woman at the farm.

Cheryl ignored the question, continuing to appear agitated. Finally, she blurted out, "Can you help me or not? I need to be moved along, out of the country, back to the U.S., I mean."

"Yes, dear," Blanco answered, forgetting his own question. "It will take time. In the meantime you need to work the fields, become a believer. These things take time," he said.

"Please hurry," she implored.

"I'll do my best. Be calm," he answered. Blanco found her exhausting to deal with at the moment.

There was a knock at the door of the study, and a small Indian boy came in and whispered to the minister that he had a very important telephone call. Father Blanco nodded. Looking at Cheryl he said, "Please, Pedro here will take you to your quarters. You can get cleaned up, rest, and we'll speak again later or tomorrow. For now, I ask you again to please remain calm. We'll work this out." He then led her to the door.

"Oh, thank you. I feel so much better. Thank you," the woman said, pumping his hand with the enthusiasm of a political candidate. "Thank you again," she said.

"Yes, yes, you're welcome. Go rest now," Father Blanco urged, trying to get rid of her as politely as possible. "Just go with Pedro," he said, closing the door as they left and quickly locking it.

The minister picked up the receiver of the telephone on his desk, pressed a blinking light, and said, "Yes?"

"I've been trying to contact you," a voice said. Father Blanco recognized the voice as that of Raul Cordova Mendoza, a.k.a. Felix the Cat.

"I'm sorry," the minister said. "I've been busy. We had a new arrival today. She's a bit of a handful."

"Never mind that, I need to put an airplane down on the landing strip. The Americans have added people in the field to track my shipments. And there is someone else running around the countryside with something I want," Mendoza sputtered.

"I thought you handled some security issues recently," Blanco said inquisitively.

"I did. That matter has been resolved. A woman who came to make trouble for me is dead," Felix said.

"I see," Father Blanco responded.

"Now a friend of that woman has shown up and involved herself in my business. My sources in the police confirmed to me her existence, and my people are looking

for her. Some other men are looking for her, too,"
Mendoza said.

"Really?" Blanco said. "Well, the new woman I have
here may interest you," the minister said smugly.

"You have her? How? Where is she? Where did you
find her?"

"Actually, she found me," the minister said with an air
of mystery.

"Has the woman discussed my property?"

"Not specifically. I am not sure she has it. She rambled
on about a friend being killed and people being after her,"
Blanco said.

"I want her. I want my property. I paid for it. Where is
my property?" Mendoza yelled into the phone.

"I don't know the answer to that yet. Have patience,
my friend. We don't want to frighten her. She knows of the
underground," the minister said.

"How much does she know about the underground?"
Mendoza asked.

"Probably not as much as she thinks. She was nosy. It's
not a problem. That issue is containable," the minister said.

"*Idiota*!" Mendoza screamed into the phone. "You deal
with that. I'm concerned with the other matter. I will hold
you responsible if our arrangements are compromised!"

Now fearing the wrath of Mendoza, Father Blanco took
on an air of obedience. "I will attend to things." Mendoza
financed his underground. Blanco could not afford to
anger him.

"Be very careful. The two men looking for her, the ones
asking about my business," Mendoza said, "are
dangerous."

"Who are they?" asked Blanco.

"They are Americans, very resourceful and ruthless."

"Are they DEA? Where did they come from?" Blanco asked.

"I don't know," he answered bluntly. "No more talking on the phone. We will meet soon. I'll be in touch. And fix your problems!"

Blanco now knew he had something the *cocainero* wanted, the woman. He just had to figure out what was going on and where he might inject himself into the profit line. Mendoza disliked any disruption of business. However, he always paid good bonuses to those who expedited matters or resolved setbacks.

Cheryl settled into the dormitory and tried to calm down. She hoped Father Blanco understood her need to get to safety. She was nervous about not being able to move on more quickly to another location.

"You a newbie?" a voice asked from a cot across from hers. "I'm Connie. What's your name, honey?

"Me?" Cheryl asked. "I'm Cheryl. I'm just passing through," she said.

"Uh huh, yeah, we all are. I've been here a year. Did he promise you a passport and a new life?" the woman queried.

"Yes, it's what he does," Cheryl said.

"Only when it suits him," Connie said.

"I'm not sure what you're getting at. This minister helps women in need," Cheryl said.

"Listen, sweetheart, I know how long I've been here," Connie shot back with an edge in her voice.

"No, women only stay here a few weeks. I know, I know the underground system," Cheryl insisted.

"But you don't know Blanco," she said. "Some women get shuttled through to make it look legit. Others get shipped off for other uses, and the rest of us are just inventory," she said.

"What do you mean? What other uses?" Cheryl asked.

"Blanco sells off young, pretty women as brides to Asians, Middle Easterners and for other business uses, whatever Mendoza wants or needs," Connie said.

"Mendoza?" Cheryl asked, knowing she heard the name before.

"Yeah, the big guy," Connie continued.

"No, no, you're mistaken," Cheryl insisted.

"We'll see. Or rather, you'll see. Actually, I don't think you have too much to worry about. It's the younger ones who get shipped out by Mendoza. Like me, you're probably too old for his needs," she said.

"You say you've been here a while?" Cheryl asked.

"About a year," Connie said.

"You don't seem bothered, kind of …"

"Accepting?" Connie said, finishing the sentence.

"Well, yes," Cheryl remarked.

"My ol' man beat me, took whatever money I had and would never let me go anywhere. Here I'm left alone as long as I do my work … and the weather is good. It beats a trailer park and a drunk with a heavy fist," Connie said.

The two women sat in a corner and talked late into the night. Connie explained the layout of the farm and cautioned Cheryl about wisecracking with Father Blanco or his people. She advised Cheryl not to ask a lot of questions.

"It's safer that way. Get some sleep, we'll talk more tomorrow."

Cheryl sat down and tried to think things through. This wasn't what she expected. She remembered hearing Mendoza's name before. Patty told her he was the head man. Patty said the drug dealers in Minnesota referred to him as their ultimate boss when she and Gary originally met with them.

Ten

Frank, Eddie and Rafael set up a small camp in a clearing off the road. Rafael hid the truck in the bush and positioned it for an easy getaway, with the back end tucked in among the brush and out of sight. He wasn't taking any chances. Rafael just wanted to be ready.

"We need a plan," Eddie said as he and Frank took inventory of their weapons. Rafael took stock of their other supplies and just listened. Rafael brought a variety of canned foods, bottles of water and a sack of fruit. Neither Frank nor Eddie asked where he found the food. Like the truck, it was just there.

Frank thought back to the guards he saw along the perimeter of the fields and compound at Blanco's farm. While the guards at the farm appeared to be easy pickings, Mendoza's men were sure to be around somewhere soon. Those guys would pose a more formidable threat. And, Frank thought, he still wasn't exactly sure yet what he was dealing with down on the farm. They needed to know if Cheryl was there before they went charging down the hill into a possible volley of oncoming gunfire.

"You're right. I want to see Blanco's holy hideaway one more time. Get some rest," Frank ordered.

"I'll go with you," Eddie offered.

"No, I'll move faster alone," Frank said.

"All right, move quietly on that ridge," Eddie cautioned his new partner. "Sudden movements make the birds and animals react and give away your position."

Frank nodded, only half listening as he pushed a pistol into his belt and took a rifle from the back of the truck. He wanted to be ready for anything.

"Listen to me," Eddie said emphatically. "You were a street cop. I'll bet in your world things that seemed out of place drew people's attention, either your attention or the attention of the people on the street around you."

Frank nodded.

"It's the same thing here in this jungle. Someone out there will be reading the sounds and sights. Birds screeching when they should be quiet, branches bent when no animals have been around, these are the sounds and visuals of this street, and you need to be aware of them. Move slowly until you get used to the environment around you," Eddie added, "and keep that dog quiet. He'll sense things long before you."

"I understand. I'll be careful," Frank conceded. "Thanks."

While the two men debated theories, the radio Frank had taken from the Jeep in back of Hector's crackled to life again with the sounds of static. He gathered up some supplies and quietly left the camp with Dutch. Frank found the viewing point where they had stretched out earlier. He scoped out the farm with the night vision goggles he took from Quintana.

The main house was dimly lit. Frank saw people moving around inside, just figures moving from one room to another. Up on a knoll behind the house was a smaller building with a steeple. Above the main door was a window cut out in the shape of a cross. It had the look of a church, probably used for group services. There were no lights on inside the small building.

Alongside the fields there were two open-air huts on stilts, one building for men and another for women. The women's building was a little larger than its twin. The walls on both stood three-quarters high and reached up to tightly thatched roofs. Inside the huts were spaces broken into several rooms with about ten cots to a room.

At the very end of the main floor of each building there appeared to be small chapel. Frank saw an altar, some religious statuary and several rows of benches. Inside each building there were small lights shining, and Frank saw people milling about and others stretched out on the cots.

While the people in the huts prepared for a night's rest, Frank observed the guards walking their posts around the encampment. They were armed with rifles and side arms. These guys were a little better armed than the men he spotted earlier. It was a small force.

That's curious, Frank thought to himself. *What does a minister need these guys for?*

Frank patted his dog's head. "Let's be quiet, Dutch. We're heading down for a look-see." Slowly, and with Eddie's words of caution ringing in his ears, he proceeded down from the hill into the crop field and advanced toward the huts. The crops in the field gave him good cover, allowing him to move quickly toward his objective. At the end of one of the huts, not quite out in the open, he counted four guards.

When two of the guards headed out to the farthest points of their perimeter, Frank and Dutch dashed from their hiding spot in the crop field, quietly slid between the two dormitories and hid behind some boxes. Frank peered out from between the two buildings and saw the guards calmly walking back to the starting points of their patrols. He had not been detected.

Frank and Dutch slipped behind one of the buildings to the side facing the jungle. No guards here. The jungle side was completely unprotected. Either there was no escape through the jungle, or there was nothing coming out of it to fear.

Frank stood still and listened. From one building came the sound of male voices. In the other building he heard the sound of female voices. He slipped along the jungle side of the women's hut and looked for places to peer in.

Through a broken slat in the wall of the building, he spied three women sitting around talking and folding freshly laundered clothes. Farther down along the building, through another break in the slats, he saw a woman sitting alone. Frank froze. It was Cheryl. She was older — hell, he was older — but it was her. He couldn't just jump up and call to her. They hadn't seen each other in years. He didn't know if she was here against her will or voluntarily. He had to think. In his mind he heard Eddie cautioning him about making snap judgments in the jungle.

Then Frank saw a door open into the hut, and a man walked in with a dinner tray.

"Tell Father Blanco I want to leave," Cheryl said loudly. "I want to go, just ask him to get me to Limon. I'll make my way from there. I don't want his help anymore," she told the man.

The man put the tray down, and Frank clearly saw a handgun stuffed into his belt. "You ain't goin' anywhere, honey," the man said. "Just get comfortable. *Senor* Mendoza is coming to see you. If you're lucky, you'll get a new home with a rich man in some exotic place. Get bitchy, and you'll wind up like your friend, dead," he said.

Cheryl jumped at him, but he pushed out his palm and hit her in the shoulder, driving her down onto the bed.

"I got orders not to get rough with you, missy. Try something stupid again and, well, orders get changed as needed," he said.

The man left, and Cheryl slumped onto a cot. She started to cry.

Instinctively, Frank wanted to jump to her defense. He restrained himself. He'd see that guy again. Frank was sure of it. He crouched down in the darkness outside the dormitory hut and waited. He waited until everyone quieted down and started to drift off to sleep.

Finally, all the lights in the two dormitories went out. Frank gazed across to the big house and saw it was dark as well. He waited a little longer and just listened. He listened for the sounds of the night. All he heard was the breeze rustling through the crops and a few jungle birds in the distance. The sounds soon settled into a pattern. Over and over, the same nature sounds repeated. It was all he heard.

Frank hoisted himself up over a rail onto the porch of the hut and slipped into the room where Cheryl was sleeping. He crept up to her and put his hand over her mouth, and her eyes shot open wide. She tried to scream but couldn't.

"Shh!" Frank commanded as he let her eyes focus on him. "Shh, I won't hurt you. Please calm down," he whispered.

He felt Cheryl's attempts to scream stop, and a strange look came over her face. She was assessing his features and thinking. She began to show signs of recognition. She knew this man.

"Can I take my hand away? Will you be quiet?" Frank asked.

She nodded.

"If you scream, we're both dead. Do you understand? I'm here to help you, to really help you," Frank whispered.

She nodded again. Frank sensed he got through to her and took a chance on trusting his instincts. He listened for a second and heard nothing. Slowly, he pulled back his hand. Cheryl sat up in the bed immediately and stared at him without speaking. She tilted her head to one side in recognition of the man sitting before her.

"Frank?" she whispered. "Frank Reardon? Is it you?" she asked softly.

"Yes," he answered.

"What are you doing here? Where did you come from?" she asked. "It's been years!"

He saw from her expression that a thousand memories from her youth, their youth, were rushing through her mind.

"How can this be?"

He cut her off before she could ask more questions.

"Later for all that, do you want to get out of here? I can get you out and home safe. Yes or no?" he said.

"Yes, yes," she answered.

"Good, who was the guy in here earlier? What was he talking about, going to some exotic place?" Frank asked.

"Oh, my God," she said. "He's in charge of all the guards. Frank, I'm so frightened. He works with Father Blanco," she sputtered.

"I know a bit about Blanco," Frank said.

"He was someone I turned to for assistance with abused women. I help them," she said. "Only now I think he's involved with sending women to far-off places as part of some sort of slave trade. One of the other women here told me about it. He's mixed up with a drug dealer named Mendoza and ..."

Frank cut her off.

"I know about Mendoza, too." The problem of the other women would have to wait until later, Frank thought.

"How'd you get down here? How did you get to this place?" he asked.

"I came through the underground for abused women looking for my friend Patty. I've been sending women in need to Father Blanco for a while. It was the only way I could find Patty. Her boyfriend was killed by these drug dealers. He was trying to sell something to them," she said.

"And she wanted to complete the sale and stole your identity to come down here and do it, right?" Frank asked.

"Yes," Cheryl said with amazement. "How did you know?"

"We'll get into the details later. First, Patty's dead."

Cheryl gasped and put her hand to her mouth, blocking any more sounds. Then she pointed at Frank's waist.

"You've got a gun," she said, "and Patty's dead? I was afraid of that."

Frank ignored the comment about the gun.

"She's in a morgue in Limon. She was initially identified as you," Frank said. "Now she's a Jane Doe. The cops dragged me in thinking I killed her because they discovered we, you and I, were friends," Frank said. "I convinced the cops she wasn't you. So after I was cut loose, I started looking for you and the trail led me here."

"This is crazy, I am so confused," Cheryl said. "Patty stole my passport. That's why I needed the underground to get me in and out of the country. The police will think I'm involved with drug dealers. I'm stuck here," she said.

"You need to trust me," Frank said. "I can help."

"How?" she asked.

As Frank started to speak, he heard the voice of the man from earlier in the night bellow from down the hall of the hut. "What's going on? Who's here?"

"Trust no one, only me. I'll be back," Frank whispered, as he touched her lips with his finger. "No one, only me," he repeated. "I'll be back." He slipped out a window and into the jungle brush a few yards away.

From under the bushes he saw a light come on in the area of the hut where Cheryl's slept. He heard the man's voice ask, "Who were you talking to?"

"A nightmare," Cheryl said, feigning grogginess. "I was having a nightmare. I just want to go home," she repeated in the same pleading voice as before. "Please let me go home!"

"Look, missy, don't keep me up all night with this whining crap. Get some sleep, do your work around here, and we'll all be a lot happier," the man said. "Understand?"

Soft, fluffy clouds moved across the sky and intermittently blocked out the moon. The field between the buildings and the main house was illuminated off and on as the clouds passed overhead. Frank waited for a dark period and quietly scampered across the field to the front of the house. He and Dutch crept under the steps of the hut's stilts and waited for the sky to go dark again before they moved. Frank made his way up the stairs and to a window on the left side of the porch. He slid the screen up and slipped into Father Blanco's study.

Frank needed information. He needed to know what was scheduled to happen at the farm. He was careful not to touch or remove anything in the room. Father Blanco's study was a large, comfortable room with leather chairs, couches, wall hangings and a huge desk. It was a man's desk, dark wood and expansive. Frank stood behind the piece of furniture. It was made for the comfortable passage of the many long hours needed to manage a profitable venture such as this farm.

There were neat piles of papers, folders and a Bible. Tucked in a corner of the desk blotter was a small stack of pink paper messages. Frank tugged them from the corner of the blotter, and right on top was one with the words "Mendoza, landing on Thursday afternoon." This was it, the information he needed. The big man was coming in two days. Cheryl was safe until Mendoza's arrival. Frank had to be ready and in place before the drug dealer showed up at Blanco's farm.

Off to the side of the desk, he spotted a file folder simply marked Inventory Reports. In it were printed tables with the names of women, dates, places around the world and dollar amounts. This is what Cheryl was talking about. It appeared Blanco was shipping off women to buyers around the globe, women who came to him seeking protection. Frank pulled some paper and a ballpoint pen from his pocket and copied as much of the information as possible. Then he tucked the messages back under the same corner of the desk blotter. He made sure the pink message sheets were in the corner of the desk pad exactly as he had found them.

Frank quietly climbed out of the window of the main house and headed back under the stairs. He and Dutch slipped past the huts and back into the crop fields. As he approached the camp, he could smell fresh coffee brewing.

Back with Eddie and Rafael, Frank got right down to business. He told Eddie they had to launch a rescue mission for Cheryl. They needed a firing spot from which to scatter the guards. Eddie looked at him askance.

"No sniper work, I promise," Frank said. "I need you to provide cover for me."

Eddie nodded and listened to Frank elaborate on what he wanted. He liked the new planning Frank. His friend was more strategic now.

"Rafael, I want you to set up an escape route to the Celtic Mistress. I left it at the docks I usually use. You know where, right?" Frank said. "You'll stay here and use these maps. Devise a route for speed."

"You trust him?" Eddie questioned.

"We've had this conversation before. Remember, Rafael? You've got nowhere to go. I already made it clear to people you're with me. You shouldn't expect any compassion from Felix Mendoza. You're simply unfinished business for him, if we don't finish him first," Frank said.

Rafael nodded reluctantly.

"I understand, *senor*. I understand."

"Good, now I need to know what's in the jungle behind the main house and buildings we saw from up on the ridge overlooking Blanco's farm. Why are there no guards on that side of the farm?" Frank asked.

"Somewhere past the jungle is an old logging camp," Rafael said. "It hasn't been used for years. It's not used for anything, and nobody goes there," he said.

"Good to know," Frank said.

As the team planned to return to the farm, the radio Frank took from the mercenary in town screeched to life. "Calling Quintana's radio, respond," the box squawked. "Calling Quintana's radio, respond."

"That's interesting," Frank said. "They are just calling his radio, not him," he said.

"They found him and saw what you did to him. They know you have his radio," Eddie said. "They've been calling every half hour since you left."

Then a familiar voice came across the airwaves. Eddie froze. Frank looked at him. Recognition of the voice swept over Eddie's face.

"I think that's my guy. He's here in Costa Rica," Eddie said.

Frank cautiously considered his next step.

"We're out-gunned if you plan on going up against Mendoza," Eddie said. "You know that."

"Answer him," Frank commanded. "Set up a meet for me. You handle the back-up."

"Back-up?" Eddie asked. "You trust me?"

"Yes," Frank said.

The two men shook hands and smiled at each other.

Eleven

The next morning Cheryl woke up and the first thing she saw was Connie standing in the room. She was staring down at her.

"I'm going, too," she said.

"What?" Cheryl said, still groggy.

"I heard you last night talking with that guy. I don't care who he is, where he came from, or where he takes us. I just want to get out of here, too." Connie demanded.

"You don't understand, I don't think I can do that," Cheryl said.

"I don't think you can afford not to do it, Cheryl. If I don't go, you don't go. Believe me, I can and I will make trouble for you," Connie said.

Cheryl thought for a moment. She was confused. She knew Frank would not debate with her about Connie. She had to stall her.

"I'll try," Cheryl said.

"No, your boyfriend said he'd be back for you. When you go, I go. It's that simple. Say yes, or I blow the deal now. It's that simple," Connie said. "We all go or we all stay, him included. Just tell him that. He'll understand. I know men," she said.

Cheryl stared up at Connie. She knew there was no way to stop her, and there was no way to warn Frank. She had no other choice.

"All right, when he comes for me, you leave too," she conceded.

Connie smiled. "Always best to start the day off with a good decision. Now let's eat. You can tell me all about this guy," Connie said, smiling.

Frank and Eddie climbed down the mountain and trekked slowly through the jungle. They kept the path to the camp in their sight but chose not to use it. If they were spotted on a path, someone might be able to find their base camp and Rafael. It was smarter to push slowly through the brush and stay out of sight. When the two men reached the road at the bottom, they hiked back toward town for a mile or more. Then they started to hitchhike, making it impossible for anyone stopping to pick them up to determine what their point of origin was on the road. At the same time the two Americans could see if they were being followed.

Eddie had answered a radio call for Quintana. Neither he nor the caller identified themselves, but each knew the other. In clipped, short sentences, they agreed Frank and the caller would meet at Hector's Restaurant, where Frank had dropped-kicked the commando in the back alley.

Frank went directly to Hector's and sat at the bar. He spotted a man sitting alone at a table. The man had to be Greco, the man he came to meet. Greco wore the same type of camouflage as the man Frank overpowered in the alley.

Slowly, Frank withdrew from a sheath on his belt the commando knife he had taken from the man he had jumped in the back alley. He wrapped the weapon in a napkin and gave it, along with some coins, to a waiter and ordered him to put it on the table in front of Greco. The waiter looked across the room at Hector, who nodded for him to comply. After the waiter delivered the knife, Greco instructed him to invite Frank to his table.

Frank sat down and Greco immediately said, "That knife belonged to a good man, or so I thought." Greco never touched the blade. It was still lying where the waiter had placed it.

"I am sure he's a good man. I thought he'd want it back. I didn't give him any chance," Frank said.

"Neither would an enemy," Greco said, not feeling very forgiving toward his employee. "He should have been prepared for surprises. Keep the knife. It's the spoils of war, albeit a small one between the two of you."

"Tell me about Blanco," Frank finally said.

"We can start there, but you need to know a whole lot more, and so do I. For starters, I need to know about the woman you're chasing," Greco said.

"After we start with Blanco," Frank insisted.

He liked this man. Greco was direct and had an air of supreme confidence. *There just might be a way to get out of this mess and save Cheryl,* Frank thought.

"This guy Father Blanco is really a two-bit con man named Kenneth Auger, a.k.a. Kenny Auger, a.k.a. Kenneth Martin, a.k.a. Kenny Martin. He was released from a New York state prison a few years back where he was doing a stretch on a forgery rap. After he was released from prison he got lost in the world of the Amish in Pennsylvania and later Ohio. While he was with those people, it was real easy for him to create a new identity for himself. He figured starting over in a world that shunned any interaction with the government, where paper trails tended to be weak at best, was an unexplored opportunity," Greco said.

"He hooked up with the Pennsylvania Amish under a false name. He called himself Kenneth Martin. Drifting from job to job, from one Amish farm to another in Pennsylvania for about a year, he solidified his new alias without the need for any paperwork. Then he drifted to Ohio where he parlayed his new Pennsylvania Amish 'credentials' into a life there. Once he was firmly entrenched in Ohio, he left the Amish and joined the less strict Mennonites. As Kenneth Martin, formerly Amish turned Mennonite, he finagled a Social Security card and obtained a driver's license. All of this secured his Kenneth Martin alias. Being a Mennonite and formerly Amish, he was easily accepted as one of those people who tended to lack the traditional government identifications and such. Traditional verifications of identities of the Amish and Mennonites are often lax in small towns. Now known as Kenneth Martin, armed with a driver's license and other trappings, he moved through their society as a new man and back into traditional society," the agent said.

"Think about it, who would question his earlier lack of credentials? He used to be Amish, right?" Greco continued. "By walking away from the Amish congregation into the Mennonites he, in essence, laundered himself. As a means of creating a new identity, it was pure genius," Greco continued.

"But why?" Frank asked. "It seems like an awful lot of work over a long period of time to build a new name.

"Good question. Unfortunately, we're not sure. He only popped up on our radar recently. He may have been planning a scam for some time. If that's the case, he's demonstrating a new sense of patience. It appears he's become a long haul player. He never attempted anything as ambitious as this farm operation before," Greco said.

"How'd he get set up down here so comfortably?" Frank asked.

"Well, as the saga of Kenny Auger, a.k.a. Kenny Martin, continues, he secured an American passport with his new identity and drifted into Mexico as a Mennonite. At this point, all his identification became foreign based. Standards for such things, new driver licenses and such, are considerably lower in Mexico than the U.S.," Greco went on.

"What about the farm here? You haven't said anything about his layout. Where'd he get the finances for a big spread up in the hills?" Frank pressed eagerly. "How does a small-timer fund that place?"

"Oh, yeah, his farm," Greco chuckled. "It isn't really his. He finessed control of it. The property belongs to some do-gooder old lady in San Diego. He conned her. It seems she was married to a guy with tons of money, and he used to beat her pretty bad. He died, and she inherited the fortune and wanted to do something for other abused women. At this point, Kenny Auger showed up on the scene. How he found her is unclear, but he wooed her and whispered sweet nothings in her ear. He sold her on the idea of building a place, something secret and private. Before you know it, he has property in Costa Rica for his religious compound to help battered women. However, the conditions are that the old lady stays away, he gets to operate his ministry in what he describes as a quiet way," Greco said.

"How do you know about this?" Frank asked.

The old lady has a son who's been screaming to any law enforcement agency he can find. When we heard Kenny was teaming up with Felix Mendoza, we started to build a file on him," Greco said. "We believe he's helping Mendoza by allowing him access to the property, sort of a drug running way station in Central America. We've tracked Mendoza. He gets to put down a plane in Kenny's quiet place and wait out any trouble that may be ahead between the farm and the border. We haven't been able to get a direct line on the drugs. They get off-loaded and reloaded out of sight of the satellites we're using. And, the big problem is that we haven't connected Kenny to any illegal activities," Greco said.

"No connection has been made yet?" Frank asked in disbelief. Greco was confirming everything Rafael had told him about the farm and Mendoza.

"Not yet. Right now, he's simply someone who associates with Mendoza. If we pop him, he'll just scream he's providing spiritual counseling to the big guy," Greco said.

"That's crap, and you know it," Frank said. "You know these guys are connected at the hip."

"Yes, so you prove it for us," Greco challenged. "We have no reason to swoop down on him. We believe Auger saw an opportunity to build his farm and underground railroad stop and at the same time offer services to the criminal element throughout the Caribbean. Proving it is our big problem," Greco added.

"What about the phony identities and the money?" Frank asked. What about the Mendoza planes that put down there?

"All of the stuff we know of takes place off U.S. soil, not a federal crime. The Social Security card isn't enough for us to cross a border," Greco said. "And the other foreign governments either lack the interest or resources to go after him. Besides, Auger's and Mendoza's spending of money in foreign countries isn't something those governments want to deter. They see it as a benefit to their economy," Greco said. "As for the planes, we have, as you cops say, no probable cause."

"Auger's done nothing in Costa Rica?" Frank questioned.

"Oh, he has prospered in Costa Rica. Not in a flashy way, though. By using yet other new identities, we believe he has filtered money out to fund apartments in Paris, a boat in the Mediterranean and a line of credit at a casino in Malaysia. Those are all places where he has never committed, and probably never intends to commit, any crimes. In those places he is a quiet, rich citizen of the world. But in Costa Rica, he is a hood linked up with Mendoza, who we believe has killed people, and probably will kill again."

"What about trafficking in women, the kidnapping of these women? I'm told he's into some sort of white slave trading operation," Frank said.

Greco looked at him and smiled. Where would a retired Bridgeport cop come across that kind of information, Greco asked himself. Aikens was right, Frank was more than he originally thought. Rather than inquire about his source of information, Greco simply said, "Rumors. We can't prove a thing on that score."

"Really?" Frank asked. "Look at this," he said, handing over a piece of paper he extracted from his pocket that had the information about the sale of the women, and the men who were their buyers.

"What's this?" Greco asked, looking at it.

"Names, dollar amounts and places," Frank said.

"Where'd you get it?" he asked.

"I swooped down. You should try it sometime," Frank said, referring to Greco's earlier comment.

"You copied all this?" he asked.

"Yes, I did," Frank answered. "I slipped into his house and poked around. With a little more time, I'll bet a lot more information could be found," he said.

"It's useless," Greco said, still holding the information in his hand. "All you have here is a bunch of handwritten notes. You can't prove any of this stuff, and it is highly unlikely we'll ever see the real documentation of this."

"But yet, you're interested in the names here," Frank said, watching him hold onto the list.

Greco smiled. "Aikens said you were good. I know these buyers, every one of them is a world class asshole," he said. For emphasis he added, "Every single one of them. They are all very dangerous."

"They all own a kidnapped woman," Frank said.

"That may be true. We just can't prove any of it in a court, any court," Greco said.

"You don't strike me as a guy who cares a great deal about the court system. Am I wrong?" Frank asked quizzically. "When I was a detective, information was the coin of the realm. If you had it, legal or otherwise, you moved to the next level in the investigation. Worrying about proving something in court came later. Tell me it's different in your world."

Greco chuckled.

"Tell me about the woman that drew you into this affair. Who is she? What's her connection to you?" Greco asked, trying to get the details he and Aikens lacked about Frank's relationship with Cheryl and her relationship to Patty and their dead freelancer Gary back in the States.

"We'll get to that. I'm still a bit confused. What exactly is a secret military-type force doing down here if you don't have a specific mission?" Frank asked.

"We're in a holding pattern, that's all I can say for now," Greco said.

"Well, I'm going back in. I have to get Cheryl out," Frank said.

"Yes, your lady friend. Tell me about her," Greco pressed.

"She's a friend from the past, and she's stuck on Blanco's farm. She came down here and got sucked into a mess involving Mendoza and drug running. The cops in Limon thought I killed her, but it was a case of mistaken identity. I have to get her away from Blanco and Mendoza and out of the country," Frank said.

"What do you want from me?" Greco asked, never offering to fill in any blanks about what he knew of the dead woman.

"Firepower," Frank said.

"I'm limited in what I can do," Greco said. "I can't go onto the farm, not just yet. I can provide backup on the open road. If you get in and out, I'll be there to play Good

Samaritan when you come racing down the road from the farm," Greco said.

"I'll take it," Frank said.

The two men shook hands and smiled at each other.

"So if you won't go in shooting, just what are you really here for?" Frank pressed.

"Life is a waiting game," Greco said with a smile. "I'm waiting for the right time to move in and snatch Padre Blanco and Mendoza. I want Mendoza, but I'll settle for the priest, minister, whatever the hell he is this week."

"Yeah, well, wait all you want for them. You just better be on that road waiting for me when I need you," Frank shot back.

"Count on it," Greco said.

As Frank turned to leave, he heard Greco call out, "Reardon, the knife." He waved his open hand over the commando knife Frank had presented to him at the beginning of their talk.

"That's not mine," Frank said. "It belongs to your guy."

"No," Greco said. "It's the spoils of war. It's your knife now. My guy will understand that. Take it."

Frank looked at him and then looked at the knife. He bent over the table and picked up the weapon.

"Just be on that road," he said.

Frank left Hector's restaurant and drifted down the street. He needed to think before he reunited with Eddie.

Greco watched Frank walk farther and farther away from the restaurant. When he felt the cop had traveled enough distance from Hector's, he withdrew a satellite telephone from inside his backpack and called Aikens.

Aikens answered immediately. "He just left," Greco said. "He seems focused on rescuing the woman. Apparently he's already been inside Blanco's camp and has spoken to her."

"She's what drew him into this affair. It doesn't surprise me. More importantly, does he know about the disc and how it fits into our drug operation investigation?" Aikens asked.

"The disc never came up," Greco said. "He's going back to Blanco's farm."

"When?" Aikens asked.

"He didn't say. We'll speak again."

"If he sneaked into the compound and made initial contact with the woman, he probably didn't have time to get the whole story," Aikens theorized. "For the moment, that works in our favor. Let's not discuss the disc until we see what he learns on his own. I suspect and hope the woman still believes the disc is genuine."

"I told him he was on his own at the farm, but pledged support on the road home," Greco said.

"Fine, let's see what he can do on his own. Just remember, we have no jurisdiction on Blanco's farm," Aikens said.

"Understood," Greco said, signing off. To himself he muttered, "No jurisdiction *yet*."

Frank made his way down the road. When he thought it was safe, he slowly looked back down the street toward Hector's and then turned a corner. Greco wasn't following him. He needed a phone. He needed to find more of the missing pieces to the puzzle of Cheryl, Blanco, Mendoza and these guys from the United States. Frank didn't believe Greco and company were just sitting around waiting for a jurisdictional opportunity.

Twelve

At an Internet café at the end of a side street in the same village as Hector's restaurant, a disinterested counter worker perused a newspaper, occasionally selling a phone card to someone making their weekly or monthly call to *el Norte*. Frank bought a phone card and telephoned Derrick Hines, the young man from the American Embassy. Derrick barely said hello before he started asking Frank questions rapid fire.

"Derrick, listen to me," Frank said.

The embassy man rambled on.

"Derrick, listen to me," Frank said again.

Derrick never paused. He continued on about the role of the embassy in police matters involving American citizens.

"Derrick, patch me through to the State Department in D.C. immediately!" Frank commanded.

Derrick went silent.

"Listen to me," Frank said, "just patch this call through and get off the line or I'll have you shipped to the worst Third World rathole I can find. Do you hear me?"

"Yes, sir," Derrick said. "Hold on."

The next voice Frank heard was a Washington receptionist.

"United States Department of State, may I help you?"

Frank asked to be connected to the security office.

"I am on an unsecured open line outside the United States and need to be patched through to a cell phone in a scramble mode. Do you understand?" Frank asked the security officer answering the call.

"Understood, code clearance, please," the voice said.

"Red 84K"

"Yes sir, please hold. Be advised this is a one-time use code. After your call clearance, code Red 84K will be disassociated from this service and permanently deactivated for the number you are calling. Your party will have to personally issue you a new code for any future calls."

"Understood," Frank said.

"Please hold."

Every cop had a few, very private investigative aces he treasured. Frank's was a contact at the Department of State. He used the relationship sparingly. The contact was always helpful, though sometimes in strange ways.

Frank assumed Derrick was still on the line, waiting to see what he could discover. That problem would disappear. Anyone else with an open phone on the line was about to hear a screeching, painful, high pitch sound.

"Hello," a voice said after the squelch and then a series of clicks. "How is the weather in your area?" the voice asked.

"Getting warmer," Frank said. "I'm trying to help an old friend, and things are getting complicated. People here have different objectives, and there are people around with secrets," Frank said cryptically.

"The people who oppose you are ruthless. Be careful. Others you have met do have different objectives, but do not let that concern you," the voice said.

"These other people have indicated to me they want to help," Frank said.

"They have their objectives. It is, however, safe to consider them allies," the voice continued. "You are a man who values loyalty. So do the people befriending you," the voice said.

"What else can you tell me?" Frank pressed.

The voice chuckled. "Please note the time now. In forty-eight hours, your new access code will be LL159." Then Frank heard a click.

Todd Hickey, the young man Aikens banished to Central America, had latched himself onto Derrick and was learning fast about how covert teams worked in the field. When Frank ordered Derrick off the phone, Todd stayed on an extension. He didn't hear any of the conversation with the person Frank called. The squelch took care of that. He did, however, hear the conversation that led up to Frank being connected with that party and understood it related to a security network. Todd didn't know who Frank's contact was but assumed the person was someone of high importance in government circles. Even Aikens had to appreciate the value of this information.

Later that day, on a conference call that included Greco, Aikens was quiet as Todd relayed to his boss what he had learned about Frank's secret contact in D.C.

"Interesting," Aikens said. "This Reardon obviously has a friend who is very grateful to him for something," he continued.

"Yes," Hickey went on. "Who knows what he has told this cop in the past. Sir, I was thinking, maybe I should continue the investigation to find this person in Washington. After all, that's where we'll be prosecuting him when he's identified and indicted for divulging information to someone not affiliated with any government agency."

Aikens ignored Hickey's suggestion and turned to Greco.

"Greco, get as close as you can to Reardon. He's becoming a bigger part of this mission. I don't want to alienate him. Understood?" Aikens said.

"Sir," Hickey interrupted. "I can be in Washington tonight."

"I get it, boss," Greco said, ignoring Hickey. "Reardon takes his time trusting people. At the same time, he is extremely resourceful. And you were right, I do like him," Greco added.

"I knew you would. You two are more alike than you may realize," Aikens said.

"Sir," Hickey pushed again.

"Hickey, continue your work in San Jose," Aikens said. Then he hung up.

Greco waited a second and finally said, "I guess you can cancel that flight to Washington, Hickey." Then Todd heard Greco hang up, too.

Frank headed toward another bar in the village to meet Eddie.

"Your friends are into a lot of things. They can also be vague about details," he said to Eddie.

"It's their nature. It was better I didn't go," Eddie said.

"Why is that?" Frank asked.

"Simple. The more people who know things, the fewer places these people have to hide. There are two ways to work with these people, right out in the open in the daylight or be in possession of information they want or want to control. Knowledge is power to them," Eddie said.

"We have knowledge of things here," Eddie continued. "They originally wanted me to keep an eye on you. Now they know about you. They'll want to know more. Are we a team?" Eddie asked.

"Yeah, we are," Frank said.

"Good. What did they tell you about what's going on?" Eddie asked.

"Not much. There was a lot of crap about them not having jurisdiction on Blanco's farm." Frank told Eddie who Father Blanco really was and how he came to Costa Rica. "I told Greco I was going back to the farm to get Cheryl. I don't care about them or their dealings with Blanco or Mendoza. That's their affair," Frank said.

"If we go back to that farm, it will stir up a hornet's nest," Eddie said.

"I have to go. Mendoza's coming in tomorrow, and who knows what will happen to Cheryl after that," Frank said.

"I'll get Rafael ready. We may need a few things," Eddie said.

Frank stayed at the bar to finish his beer. Over the concrete wall he saw a truck pull up, and a man in a black cassock stepped out. He took a seat at a table at an outdoor café. Some young people, men and women, jumped out of the back of the truck and fanned out into the stores. The driver never left the vehicle.

"Who is that man?" Frank asked the bartender, pointing to the man in the cassock.

"That is *Padre Blanco, senor*," the bartender said. "He and his missionaries come to the village every week for supplies."

Frank nodded and said nothing. *The great Father Blanco doing grocery shopping,* Frank thought.

Father Blanco sat at the table of the outdoor café and nodded piously at passing villagers. Frank ambled over, pulled up a chair and sat down across from the cleric. Without any flair, but in a manner recognized by felons around the globe, he flashed his old detective's badge. Father Blanco simply stared and said nothing.

"I'm looking for a woman I believe is traveling in Costa Rica. I think she may have made her way to your farm in the valley up in the hills. I can help her get home to the United States safely. I'd like to come up and see if she's there," Frank said.

"Women sometimes come to me for protection, sir. I can't allow people to search our home," the cleric responded as he twirled a polished wooden cross that hung around his neck.

Frank smiled and tapped the table with his badge, letting it glisten in the sunlight.

"Sir, even a poor minister like me knows that badge has no value in Costa Rica," Blanco ventured.

"Maybe not, but it has friends here," Frank said. Then Dutch appeared at his feet. The dog had disappeared into the town when he and Eddie arrived. It was his way,

Frank came to know. No matter where they went, somehow the dog always managed to show up later where they parted, wagging his tail and waiting to have his head rubbed.

"People should always have friends," Blanco said, still trying to maintain his smile. Frank thought Blanco was showing more of a smirk, but then noticed how he was looking at Dutch warily.

"Nevertheless, I would still like to visit your farm," Frank said.

"Not possible. We maintain strict privacy rules."

"I've asked you nicely," Frank pressed.

"Sir, I am trying to be polite. But even a religious man can have his patience tested," Blanco said. "Now," the self-made minister said, "I'd very much like to be left alone." With a touch of sternness, he leaned forward and quietly added, "Don't bother me again. I am warning you."

Dutch gave a guttural growl. It could not be heard beyond the table, but the minister heard it clearly. Frank smiled and slid his hand down to scratch the dog's neck. It calmed him.

Very slowly, Frank leaned over and whispered next to the man's ear.

"Kenny, you should reconsider."

Blanco stared at him wide-eyed. He cowered at Frank's use of his name.

Frank stood, snapped his fingers for Dutch to follow, and walked away and into the crowd on the street. In a few seconds Blanco could no longer see him. The minister gathered up his newspaper and called around for his missionaries to abandon their shopping and get to the truck.

"We're leaving now!" he called out. "Everyone get to the truck!" Beads of sweat were forming on the back of his neck, and he felt his heart racing.

In the truck Kenny Auger's cell phone buzzed in his pocket. Only one person ever called him on the cell phone. He knew before answering who was calling him.

"I am told there are two Americans in your area asking questions. They may show up at the farm," Mendoza said.

"Yes, I've met one," Father Blanco said as he proceeded to describe the scene in town at the café. "He called me Kenny," Blanco said. "He knows who I am. How does he know who I am?"

Mendoza was silent.

"Find them and capture them," Mendoza said, ignoring the question from the mail-order minister.

"Good, I'll have them captured and killed as soon as possible," Kenny said.

"No," Mendoza shouted. "I want them alive!"

"They may know too much," Kenny protested.

"I need to know what they know," Mendoza said. "You have your orders. Do I make myself clear?"

"*Si, senor,*" Kenny said quietly. "I understand."

"Good." The phone went dead.

Frank sat at the bar at Hector's with a cold *Presidente* beer and watched Blanco's truck roar out of the village. Eddie walked in, shifting his gaze back and forth between Frank and Blanco's truck.

"I saw you speaking to him. I gather he knows we're interested in his mountain operation," Eddie said.

Frank took a swig from the bottle and swallowed.

"He knows *now*," Frank said with a smile.

"Was that smart?" Eddie questioned.

"He's up there alone without Mendoza. He'll be nervous, and nervous people are careless people," Frank said.

"And you think having him nervous gives you an edge?" Eddie asked.

"I take them where I find them," Frank said.

"We'll have to move fast," Eddie said.

"Yes, we will," Frank agreed.

As soon as Frank and Eddie arrived at their camp and rejoined Rafael, they took inventory once again of their stock of weapons.

"What's that?" Frank asked.

"Grenades, about two dozen," Eddie said with a smile.

Frank looked over at Rafael. "Just so we're all clear about things," Frank said, "you can stay with us or leave. Decide now. I've spoken to Father Blanco, he knows we're coming in soon. And I know Mendoza is coming in soon, too. If nothing else, your relationship with him is over."

"What do you want of me?" Rafael sighed. His immediate future was clearly with Frank and Eddie.

"Backup," Frank said. "I need for you to back us up while Eddie and I do what we do best."

"Cause trouble?" Eddie asked sarcastically.

"Exactly," Frank said.

Frank described the layout of the farm, the fields where the people worked, and the large manor house where Blanco lived. He planned to slip in as he had done before, get Cheryl, make their way over to the house, and grab evidence about the selling and transporting of women around the world. That would help Greco.

"Wait a second," Eddie said. "We'll have limited time in the compound. We might not be able to locate and secure that kind of documentation. We're there to get this woman out," he said. "I suggest we keep it simple."

"We need the data. We have to shut this guy down," Frank shot back.

"Not a good idea," Eddie protested. "We're going to be traveling with a woman. We have to get in and out fast!"

"What about all the other women who were funneled through Blanco's human portal?" Frank questioned.

Eddie paused. Frank's plan was risky. But he agreed.

Several hours later, still under the night moon, Frank led Eddie to the edge of the field he crossed the first time at Blanco's farm. The two men were looking at the women's hut. Using sign language, Frank indicated Cheryl's sleeping area was above them inside the raised building. He motioned for Eddie to follow. Eddie nodded.

They climbed up the small flight of stairs and Frank crept into Cheryl's room. As he had done before, he put his hand over her mouth to prevent any screams as he woke her. Her eyes popped open and she remained silent and nodded recognition.

"Let's go, now," Frank said quietly removing his hand from Cheryl's mouth. Eddie stood guard at the door, assault rifle pointed outward.

Cheryl didn't move. "Frank, listen to me" she said quietly.

"Cheryl, we'll talk later. Please, let's go, now," Frank urged.

"One for all and all for one," a woman's voice whispered behind him.

Frank spun around and pointed his weapon at Connie standing in another doorway.

"Who the hell are you?" he demanded.

"Frank," Cheryl said. "This is Connie, she wants to come with us. She said she'll make trouble if you refuse. I had no way to warn you."

Eddie heard the voices. He peeked into the room and saw the extra woman.

"What's going on?"

"Quiet!" Frank answered.

He turned back to Connie.

"What the hell do you want?"

"I want what she wants," Connie said. "I want out of here and so does she," Connie said, flipping a blanket off a nearby bed and exposing a young woman, barely in her twenties, taking in the conversation around her. "These guys will ship this kid to God knows where," Connie continued. "You know what will happen to her. She's a prize. You know what's going on here. You're our ticket out, our only ticket out," Connie insisted.

Frank stared and thought.

Eddie had scurried in and heard Connie.

"Shit, this isn't good."

"We can't leave them here now," Frank said.

Eddie ran his fingers through his hair and rubbed his hand across his face. "How much ammo are you carrying?" Eddie asked.

Frank looked at the girl and asked "What's your name?"

"Christine," she murmured.

"Well, Christine," Frank said, "it looks like we're all getting out of here tonight."

Eddie just shook his head.

"Just listen to us, and do as we say. We'll sort out the details later. Let's go now," Frank commanded.

Cheryl touched Frank's arm and softly said, "Thank you."

The women said nothing and followed Eddie out of the hut. Frank and Dutch brought up the rear. Slowly the group moved down the stairs to toward a passageway between two buildings. Straight ahead Frank saw the crop field in the distance. He moved to the head of the group. He then signaled with his fingers to move out, single file. He directed everyone toward the field and put his finger to his lips to signal silence.

The line of escapees stretched from the hut across the killing zone almost to the crop field. They quietly moved forward. When they had nearly reached the line of crops, a string of floodlights suddenly lit up the compound.

"Stop where you stand, immediately!" Kenny ordered over a loudspeaker.

A blast of automatic weapons fire tore up a strip through the grass beside Eddie, Frank and the women. Everyone froze.

Kenny Auger stepped out of the shadows dressed in camouflage pants and a starched safari shirt with two buttoned breast pockets and shiny black paratrooper jump boots. On his belt he had a holster and a stainless steel automatic handgun with a black handgrip. Behind him were four men. They were dressed in similar clothes, only showing a bit more wear and tear.

"You two, drop your weapons," Kenny said, pointing to Frank and Eddie.

The floodlights gave the area the feel of a Texas high school football field on a Saturday night. Frank and company were midway to the goal line when Auger and his team blocked their way. Frank and Eddie looked at the women and knew their play was over. Auger's team was better armed. Both men placed their weapons on the grass and raised their hands in the air.

"Very good decision, gentlemen," Auger said as he approached.

Frank gazed into his eyes as he closed in on him. He watched his hands and the slowness of his step. Then his eyes looked past Kenny and the men behind him. In the distance he saw a few more men with their weapons trained on the women and Kenny's team of missionaries. *Everything is coming to an end,* Frank thought. *Kenny is closing up shop.*

Frank and Eddie started looking for an opportunity, any opportunity. Then they heard another burst of gunfire let loose. Just as before, another strip of grass was torn up with a line of bullets fired from a small hill on the side of the crop field. Frank and Eddie dove to retrieve their weapons. Auger moved in quickly and kicked Frank in the temple with his heavy boot. He stumbled and fell as Auger kicked him again in the back and sprawled him out on the ground.

Dutch lunged for Auger. A man behind Kenny stepped in and hit the dog in the head with the butt of his rifle. Frank saw Dutch's seemingly lifeless body fall to the ground in the darkness.

Another blast of weapons fire erupted and the lights went dark as glass sprinkled down from above.

"Move, move, keep going!" Eddie screamed, commanding the women to run for the crop field.

"Kill them," Auger ordered his men.

The men moved toward the field as Eddie and the women disappeared into the crops. With their weapons at their shoulders, they waited to fire until they sighted a target. The soldiers were experienced enough to know they might kill each other in the dark if they fired without seeing a clear target.

"No, no, don't leave me alone!" Auger screamed at his troops, countermanding his order to kill the others now escaping. "Get this prisoner inside, now!"

Frank looked up at Kenny and saw him staring down at him. Hurt and bleeding from his head, Frank chuckled at the fear he saw in Auger's eyes. Even hurt, Auger feared Frank. This was his edge.

Frank saw the rustling in the crop field slow to a stop. The lack of movement in the field confirmed to him that the group had managed to elude the pursuers. They were deep into the field and out of danger from the gunmen, who were still trying to process the conflicting orders from Kenny.

Thirteen

Eddie hustled the women through the crop field. He didn't hear any sounds from Frank's gun, and he had lost sight of Frank, too. He just kept moving. Maybe Frank was just a few minutes behind in the crop field. It was better to keep his group moving toward camp.

On the ridge Eddie met up with Rafael. He was ecstatic over his role in the group's escape.

"I took out the lights! I knew you'd escape in the darkness," Rafael said gleefully. "It worked. Wow, you should have felt that gun vibrate in my hands. I never felt anything like that before."

"Shut up," Eddie demanded.

"What? I thought you'd be happy. You got away because I shot out the lights!"

"Shut up! Frank isn't with us. He's missing," Eddie responded.

Rafael fell silent. He thought his blast of fire saved them all.

Eddie listened for any rustling in the field, the sounds of birds being disturbed in the night, coyotes racing for cover, anything. There was nothing. Everything was quiet on the trail behind them. From the ridge, Eddie saw one of the huts at Father Blanco's farm all lit up. Frank must have been captured.

Eddie led everyone to the camp and started to look around. He had to move the women. They couldn't stay here.

"Start packing, we have to get out of here," Eddie said to the group.

Cheryl, Connie and Christine moved as fast as possible, pressing to cover more ground. Rafael and Eddie switched taking the point position on the road ahead.

Back on Father Blanco's farm, Kenny's men dragged Frank into the hut where the women slept, bound his hands and ankles. He was hung by his wrists from a hook in a crossbeam of the main room. Auger nodded at a man who jammed a rifle butt hard into Frank's ribs. The pain shot up and down Frank's body.

"Not so tough now, cop," Auger said. "I guess that old badge didn't do you any good after all," he said. "Hit him again," Auger commanded.

The man repeated the blow. Frank dangled from the beam and winced, trying to regain his breath.

"Now, you and I are going to have a talk. You're going to tell me everything you know. And I mean everything," Kenny said.

Auger nodded again and the man hit Frank in the ribs even harder than before. Frank eyed the man and tried to concentrate on anything but the pain. His attacker wasn't one of Mendoza's men. He was crude and smiled when he worked Frank over. Frank also noticed the knife and scabbard he had taken from Greco's man stuffed in his attacker's belt.

Frank looked at Kenny and smiled through the pain.

"You think those new clothes are enough to graduate you from street punk status to a full blown thug? You've got a long way to go, pal," Frank said. "You're little Kenny Auger, a street hustler who forges ID cards and scams widows out of their real estate, nothing more."

Surprise and anger coursed through Auger. This cop knew too much. Kenny decided he wasn't leaving here alive.

Through the window Frank saw Father Blanco's congregation lined up on the grass. Kenny's men held them at gunpoint. They were confused, seeing a man being beaten by the guard. They didn't understand the transformation of their spiritual leader. They realized now that they were just farm workers for Kenny, nothing more. It was clear he took advantage of their simple nature and belief in a better way of life.

Kenny spent the night trying to break Frank's spirit. The cop only angered Kenny more by smiling through the beatings and refusing to answer any questions. The self-proclaimed minister wanted to kill Frank and be done with the whole affair, but he feared having to explain his failure to Mendoza.

At some point in the morning hours, Frank passed out. Kenny, tired and inexperienced in interrogation methods, simply allowed his men to rest.

Frank regained consciousness sometime later. He scanned the room and saw Kenny and his men dozing. He used the time to regain his focus and mentally push through his pain. As he was wondering what was going to happen next, he heard an airplane approaching. It had to be Mendoza. He was landing at the airstrip. Things were about to change.

Kenny stirred and jumped to his feet when he heard the engines in the air. He awakened his men with kicks to their feet.

"Get up, you fools! Get up!"

"Sounds like your boss is on his way here," Frank said wryly.

"My partner," Auger corrected.

"Partner? You think so? Listen up, Kenny-boy. Guys like Mendoza have two kinds of people in their lives, people they work for and people who work for them. You figure out where you fit in, Kenny. Ask for a partnership meeting, see what he says." Frank laughed through his pain.

Auger nodded again to his guard. One more time the man drove the end of his rifle into Frank's rib cage. Frank laughed again. Kenny didn't have the guts to kill Frank the night before, and his courage was less now with Mendoza on the way.

"What about your ministry, Kenny? What about those people out there watching you? You think those people will just farm the land and watch you leave with Mendoza? They know who he is," Frank said. "He'll kill them."

"Shut up," Kenny said, growing more confused and remembering the missionaries were still being held at gunpoint outside.

Up in the hills Eddie sneaked over to a ridge above the airstrip. Through the scope of his sniper rifle, he watched an airplane come down and make a perfect landing as dawn broke. The small runway was lit only by the early morning glow and the bare electric bulb burning in the shack at the end of the blacktop airstrip. The plane taxied right up to the shack. A Land Cruiser waited for the party to disembark from the aircraft. One man in particular seemed to be a VIP. He was dressed in a finely tailored suit. The people with him hurried ahead to open doors for him and carried his briefcase. He had to be Mendoza.

Eddie tried to formulate a plan to rescue Frank. Eddie knew any plan, even a bad plan, was better than waiting for his friend to die.

"Come with me, we need to talk," he said to Cheryl back at camp.

She rose and followed him to the edge of the camp.

"I need to know what was going on at the farm, how you got there, who came and went, what type of things Father Blanco was into, and how things were accomplished. I don't have much time, so give me the big picture and I'll ask for the details I need," he said.

Cheryl nodded and confirmed many of the things he already knew, such as Blanco funneling runaway women into a slave trade operation and Mendoza using the place as a safe haven for his drug running flights. And then she told him about her friend's boyfriend Gary. He was trying to sell Mendoza's men a computer program, and it got him killed. "Gary had some sort of disc. I told Frank about it briefly. When he showed up at the farm, things just happened too fast to explain the details," she said.

She told Eddie that Gary was killed when he tried to squeeze Mendoza's men for more money. She told him how Patty came to Costa Rica, using Cheryl's stolen identification papers, to complete the deal. Frank knew it would be easier for Patty to avoid capture and get lost in Central America or Caribbean countries by switching back and forth between the stolen identification papers and her own identification. Cheryl said she followed Patty, using the woman's underground, in an effort to stop her.

"She was ill-equipped to deal with these men, especially down here," Cheryl said. "And now she's dead! Frank told me that much. She was carrying an old photo of Frank and me that was in my passport case. That's how he became involved. The police thought I was patty when they found her body."

Eddie nodded. "Where's the disc now?"

Cheryl stood silent.

"Cheryl, the disc, where is it?" Eddie pressed.

"Frank said it was our absolute best bargaining chip and to hold onto it as long as possible," she said.

"This is it, right now. I need the disc to get Frank out," he said.

Slowly, she turned, bent over and pulled up her shirt. On her back was a taped a square of heavy gauze.

Eddie gazed at it. "You've had it there for a while," he said.

"Yes," Cheryl answered. "Even Frank doesn't know I have it. I took it from Patty's hotel room after they killed her and before the police showed up. I figured out where she hid it," Cheryl said. "It was under her mattress. She was always stuffing things under her mattress at home."

"Good. Go back to camp and don't tell anyone else about the disc. I'll be back."

Eddie moved a little deeper into the bush with the radio he used to contact Greco. After a brief conversation, Eddie went still deeper into the jungle and quietly made his way to the airstrip.

As he pressed along the footpath through the area, he heard a four-wheel drive vehicle on the nearby road. Eddie made his way to a knoll over the road and saw the small truck in the distance. The driver was alone, moving slowly through the area, looking for the fugitive's camp. Other Mendoza cohorts had to be winding through the hills in other sectors. Sooner or later, Rafael, the women and the camp would be discovered.

Slowly and silently Eddie worked his way through the jungle and down to the airstrip. He slunk into a ditch that ran alongside the runway and made his way to the shack where the airplane was tied down. He stopped about fifty yards from the plane. He heard the sounds of bugs in the jungle and the faint static of a radio coming from the shack. Through his scope he saw that the man inside the shack was still reading his newspaper. With stealth, Eddie slipped onto the runway, made his way to Mendoza's airplane, and went to work. After about thirty minutes he completed his tasks. He scurried back to the ditch, moved down alongside the runway and into the jungle. He disappeared silently as the radio static mingled with the sounds of the mosquitoes in the night.

Traveling along the footpath through the heavy woods, Eddie heard the rumble of the vehicle again. The old jungle truck traversed the pot-holed road slowly. The clank of the frame when a front wheel hit a deep pothole told Eddie that the shocks were well past their prime. No matter how he tried, the driver was unable to keep the truck silent. That was Eddie's edge.

The sniper slipped off the footpath and got down on his stomach in the middle of the same dirt road as the truck. Eddie took a shooting position at the crest of a hill. The road stretched out straight in front of him for about one hundred and fifty yards before the double rutted path took a bend to the right. Eddie fixed his homemade silencer on the front of the rifle's barrel and scanned the road through the scope. One clean tire shot was all he needed. When the truck clanged out of the bend and rolled straight toward him, Eddie would take his one clean shot.

The truck bounced down the road toward him. The metal parts of the frame rattled in the night and played harmony with the squeaky seats. The driver was trying to make time now, moving the old vehicle faster toward home. The open-air truck swung around the bend, and the headlights shot two beams over Eddie's prone body lying in the dirt.

One hundred and fifty, one hundred and twenty-five, one hundred … and then at ninety yards, Eddie's rifle spit out two rounds, which hit just below the right headlamp shining at him. There was an explosion of rubber as Eddie rolled to one side into the brush.

The driver ground the old truck, veering and bucking, to a halt. He jumped out from behind the wheel and saw the flat tire. In the dark Eddie heard him curse the blowout. The man started to retrieve the spare tire. Eddie slipped up behind him and slammed his rifle butt across his temple. Eddie heaved the man's body onto the truck bed, then tied and gagged him. He fixed the flat and slowly drove the truck to a section of brush by a cliff overlooking Auger's farmhouse. Leaving the unconscious and bound driver in the truck, he went to get Cheryl.

Eddie said nothing to the others when he arrived in camp close to dawn. Everyone was wide awake.

He approached Cheryl and spoke softly. "I need you to go back in. It's the only way to get Frank out."

Cheryl stared at him and said nothing.

"You need to trust me," he said. "I have resources," he said. "Get Frank to trust us, to trust me. Only you can do it. It's our only hope, and for you to get Frank to trust us, you have to trust me," he said. "I don't have time to explain. It's the only way to get him out of there and all of us out of here."

Cheryl nodded in agreement. "Tell me what you want me to do," she said.

At the farm, Felix Mendoza and his men strutted single file into the hut. Mendoza looked around and saw Frank hanging from the rafters in the same building where Cheryl and the other women slept. He saw the bruises on Frank. The *cocainero* boss slowly walked over to Kenny and slapped him across the face with the back of his hand.

"Who told you to do this?" Mendoza demanded.

"I loosened him up," Kenny said.

"You gave him resolve," Mendoza shot back.

Mendoza approached Frank and said, "I want the disc, and I want the woman to bring it to me."

"I don't know what you're talking about," Frank said.

Mendoza strolled over to a sideboard in Kenny's office, picked up a bottle of Havana Club rum and poured himself a drink. He took a sip and nodded to one of his men. A muscular man stepped forward and slammed his fist into Frank's kidney. Pain seared him, and his eyes filled with tears.

The drug dealer turned to Kenny and said, "When you hurt a man, make it count. Make him know you are serious. This *gringo*," Mendoza lectured Kenny as he waved the glass in his hand toward Frank, "is not someone you want to toy with very long."

Mendoza turned to his thug, nodded again, and Frank was hit by the man's club of a fist.

"*Senor*, I can do this longer than you can sustain it. You must know what I say is true," Mendoza said to Frank who stared back but was silent. Then, in the distance, a horn blared. Mendoza was distracted but kept his eyes on Frank. The horn continued to disrupt the daybreak. Mendoza's patience waned.

"What is that noise?" he yelled, annoyed by the continuous sound of the horn.

"On the ridge, *senor*! I see a truck!" a man said.

"Silence it, do it now," Mendoza ordered.

"Men are on the way," a voice responded.

Finally the sound of the horn ended. Shortly afterward, two of Mendoza's men returned sheepishly to the hut carrying a note and a radio unit. The note, addressed to "Felix the Cat," ordered him to tune to a specific radio frequency. The men told Mendoza the guard in the truck searching for the others had been overpowered, tied, and left leaning on the vehicle's horn.

Mendoza waved the note at Frank and screamed "What's this?" Turning to a subordinate, he ordered the radio frequency be found. Almost immediately, Eddie's voice was heard on the unit.

"Come in at the farm, calling the farm," Eddie called over the radio.

"Give me that," Mendoza said, grabbing the microphone. "Who is this?"

"Ah, *Senor* Mendoza, I presume," Eddie said. "I have something you want, and you have something I want."

"I'm listening," Mendoza hollered.

"Good. Let's keep this simple. I have a computer disc you want, and I have the money you paid for it. All I want is your captive. I want to trade your property for my friend," Eddie said.

"Who are you?" Mendoza asked.

"Not important," Eddie said.

Mendoza assessed matters as the others stood silent. His mind raced through the facts and analyzed all the possibilities with the speed of a computer.

"It's a deal. Send the merchandise in with the woman he came for."

Eddie paused. "Deal," he said.

"No!" Frank screamed coming to life.

"Shut him up," Mendoza said to the man who had previously hit Frank. Another kidney punch followed. Frank winced and went silent again.

Eddie ignored Frank's objections and continued to speak to Mendoza over the radio.

"When they're out of here, you will be called about where to find the money you've already paid for this product. The cash is our leverage."

"Deal," said Mendoza, greedy to reclaim his money, too.

"Send her to the main house," Mendoza said, ordering everyone to leave the hut.

Turning to Frank, Mendoza said, "It seems you'll live a little longer."

Kenny and two of Mendoza's men took Frank off the hook, cut the bindings on his feet, and hustled him to the main house. Other armed men moved the confused disciples of Padre Blanco from their position outside the hut to a clearing outside the main house.

A short time later the sound of a truck was heard coming up the main road. A guard called out that it was being driven by a woman, and she was alone. The drug boss smiled.

Cheryl brought the old truck to a halt at the steps of the main house where she had first met Padre Blanco. Crowding the steps and the porch were Mendoza's men. They leered at her. She steeled herself to appear emotionless as she passed.

"Ah, *senora*," Mendoza said as she entered the house. "Come in, where is my merchandise?" he asked without losing any time.

"I want to speak to Frank privately," she said.

"No," he said. "Where is my merchandise?"

She offered no answer.

Mendoza sighed with frustration and waved his hand toward Frank, who was sitting nearby, his hands still bound.

Cheryl leaned over and spoke softly to Frank. "Eddie says to trust him," she said.

His eyes told her he was leery.

She leaned in close and whispered softly "LL159."

Frank's eyes widened. That was his new code for his Washington connection.

"My merchandise, *senora*, I want it now," Mendoza said anxiously.

Cheryl reached under her shirt and ripped the taped disc from her back. Mendoza accepted it gleefully and pulled the tape off the plastic holder. It was a simple computer disc, but he examined it with the admiration of an art collector.

The drug dealer gave the disc to one of his men and pointed to a laptop on Kenny's desk. Without any words being exchanged, the man put down his assault weapon and popped the disc into the laptop's drive. Several command boxes appeared. He followed their directions and typed feverishly. Mendoza studied every one of the technician's keystrokes. He was ready to pounce on him if he dallied in bringing the program to life. There were a few electronic beeps, tiny lights on the computer flickered, and in an instant, an opening page for a website appeared.

"We're in," the man said simply.

"Then it works?" Mendoza questioned.

"*Si, senor*," the soldier-turned-techie said.

"Good, shut it off," Mendoza ordered.

The technician complied immediately.

"*Senora*, I can't let you go. Too many people know about my business here with Padre Blanco and you," Mendoza said.

"You won't get your money," Cheryl screamed.

"A pittance compared to what this disc will earn for me," The Cat said.

"You can't kill us," Frank said. "Too many people expect to hear from us. They'll come looking for you."

"You must know by now, *senor*, people die all different ways in the jungle. They suffer from falls, encounters with animals, random gunfire, so many things. And often there is no one to explain anything. Eventually, people forget and move on. People will forget about you," Mendoza said.

In Washington, D.C., three levels below the ground floor in the gray granite building where Aikens had read the riot act to his troops, a light on a control panel blinked, signifying activity on a dormant computer network. An analyst switched screens on his terminal and saw that the dummy network had been activated.

"Hey, look at this," the analyst said to his cubicle partner. "It went live. Then it died."

"Call the boss," his partner said, staring at the blank screen.

The section chief arrived and was immediately briefed.

"A trace?" he asked.

"The log-on was too short in time; we couldn't get a definite fix," the analyst said.

"Can we get a general geographic fix?" the boss asked.

"Possible."

"Get me everything you can, and I mean everything. Give me your best assumptions ASAP," the chief said. He picked up a phone and dialed an operator, and said "Patch me through to Mr. Aikens, wherever he is."

Within minutes Aikens was asking the same questions the computer room boss had just asked his tech team.

"Finally, we're in business," Aikens said, closing up his cell phone. He called Greco to update him.

Fourteen

Mendoza stood by the desk in the den of Father Blanco's farmhouse and smiled. Finally, he had secured his prize. The computer program worked. The new tool enabled him to monitor all of the U.S. Coast Guard interdiction forces in the Caribbean and along the Central American coastline from Panama to Mexico. Mendoza could pick the most opportune times to increase or halt his drug shipments to the United States. His drug running affairs just became a great deal more efficient. The Cat's success rate had always been fairly good. Now he was about to improve that record. That would please his business partners in South America.

Of course, they never need know how he achieved his improved shipping numbers. They would simply see his efficiencies and reward him. He smiled. His future was bright.

"Turn it on again," Mendoza barked with glee. "Let me see it again." He smiled broadly as the computer program came to life on the screen, showing maps of the Caribbean and icons representing ships and planes.

"Show me which ones are the American Coast Guard boats," he ordered his technician.

"The blue ones," the tech said, tapping each icon on the screen with the point of a pencil. "The other icons represent cargo ships, fishing boats and some large pleasure craft. And these icons," the tech said, pointing to a different shape, "are airplanes. We have different colors for private, commercial, and American military aircraft."

"Where do we go from here, and when do we leave?" Kenny asked as he followed Mendoza outside to the porch.

"We? There is no *we*," Mendoza said.

"I'm your partner. I can't stay here. The Americans know this place is a front. They'll bring the authorities soon."

"That is not my problem, *Padre*. I enjoyed the hospitality of your little airstrip. Only it now appears I may have little use for it in the future. If things calm down for you, I may come back," Mendoza said as he headed for the stairs.

"Wait! I used the women from the network to help you win favor with your customers all over the world," he hollered. "These were disposable women who served your business needs. All of these women were untraceable. I provided a valuable service. I developed a very unique concept and you used it extensively." he said.

Mendoza stopped and spun around. "Who do you think you are speaking to? Don't you ever raise your voice to me again. You're an idiot. Dealing in the women was your business. I never liked it. It was convenient at the time. Now I have what I want. I don't need your network of women. It took me a long time to get this, partly because of your mistakes," Mendoza said.

"But you took advantage of the trades," Auger repeated as he waved his book of transactions. The leather journal contained a detailed account of who went where and how much was paid to him for each woman by each client.

"Yes, I did, and I said I no longer care. Its usefulness for me has ended. I now have a better insurance policy," he said, patting his briefcase.

"What about them?" Auger said, pointing through a window at Frank and Cheryl.

"Kill them before they kill you. Maybe then, I won't have to kill you," the drug dealer sneered as he headed to his vehicle, which would take him back to the airstrip.

Kenny returned to the den and saw Frank hunched over the couch and Cheryl standing next to him. The man who worked over Frank with the rifle butt was guarding them, waiting for orders. Kenny watched Mendoza's vehicle drive away. He turned to speak to Frank but paused. He thought he heard a familiar, muffled sound. He cocked his head for a second, trying to identify it. Frank watched him strain to identify the noise. Kenny dismissed it. Frank, however, recognized the sound as the unmistakable low growl of Dutch. The dog was alive. Off in a corner under a table, the brown eyes of the junkyard dog stared out from the darkness. Frank slowly shook his head back and forth, signaling for Dutch to remain quiet and hidden, if only for a few more moments.

Kenny walked in circles in the den.

Suddenly, there was an explosion from the airfield. Smoke billowed high into the sky, and a series of smaller explosions echoed through the valley.

The guards Kenny had stationed outside the hut abandoned their posts and ran after Mendoza, choosing to try to protect the real powerbroker. Father Blanco's followers scattered into the fields and the surrounding jungle.

"Dutch, attack!" Frank screamed as he rushed the guard, hitting the man in the stomach with his shoulder and driving him into a wall. The guard slumped to the floor. Frank rolled over and got up on his feet. He kicked the guard in the rib cage as he tried to stand. The blow from Frank's boot drove the man flat onto the floor. Frank kicked him in the head and knocked him unconscious.

On command, Dutch bolted out from underneath the table and jumped at Kenny with his jaws wide open. He sunk his teeth into Auger's shoulder, and the two fell to the ground wrestling with each other. Kenny was screaming.

Cheryl cried at the sight of Dutch tearing into Kenny and of Frank viciously kicking the guard into submission. Frank quickly reclaimed his knife and withdrew it from the scabbard.

"Frank!" Cheryl screamed.

Frank spun around to see that the guard had regained consciousness and was charging him. He gripped the knife's handle tightly and drove the blade into the man's stomach. He grabbed his victim's shirt as he slumped down, looked into his eyes and watched him die.

Behind Frank, Dutch and Kenny were still rolling around the floor. The dog's growl grew more ferocious and Kenny's pleas for help more plaintive.

"Dutch, heel!" Frank ordered.

Dutch immediately backed off. Kenny bolted out the door and down the road after Mendoza, but the *cocainero* was driving fast toward the airstrip and the explosions.

"Let's go," Frank said to Cheryl as he picked up the leather book and put the knife back in its sheath.

"That explosion was Eddie," she said, grabbing a satchel bag by the desk. "He told me he wired Mendoza's airplane with grenades."

"If he's destroyed their airplane, they'll be back. Let's head this way," Frank said, pointing to the jungle behind the house. "There's an old logging camp out this way. We can double back and catch up with Eddie."

"Eddie said to meet him at camp in two hours. If we're late he said to head directly to your boat. I don't think he can hold them off for two hours alone." Cheryl said.

Then there was the sound of gunfire moving from place to place. Frank's experienced ear knew a chase was under way.

"Yes, he can. There's a small army out there he's working with," Frank said. He believed Greco's team would be on the road.

Eddie sat in the bush alongside the runway after the plane exploded and waited. The sniper smiled. He had positioned a fifty-gallon fuel drum by the fuselage and strung grenades among the other barrels during his earlier reconnaissance visit to the airstrip. He had taken aim and fired at the fuel drum. The drum set off an explosion that blew up the plane's fuel tanks. A chain reaction destroyed the other fuel drums and all of Mendoza's drugs on the twin engine Beechcraft.

Mendoza's motorcade, with armed men poking their heads up through the sun roofs of the vehicles, sped down the road and up to the wreckage of the airplane. Eddie watched them approach the burning plane. When they were within range, Eddie gave the signal and Greco's men, well hidden and dispersed around the perimeter of the airstrip, opened up with gunfire. The motorcade came to a halt, and Mendoza's men instinctively returned fire to where the first volley originated.

It was too late. After firing, Greco's men had immediately repositioned themselves to new spots. The shoot-and-run gambit kept Mendoza's men busy while Eddie retreated to move Connie, Christine and Rafael out for their escape to the *Celtic Mistress*. He counted on Frank to use the diversion of the exploding airplane for his own escape with Cheryl.

Eddie arrived back at the campsite. After precisely two hours he herded everyone out. He had to get them moving forward, away from the airstrip, the farm and anything to do with Mendoza or Father Blanco. It was too dangerous to linger any longer. He had to believe Frank and Cheryl could make it to the boat as well.

Secure for the moment up in the hills, Frank stopped momentarily in his flight with Cheryl. He saw men coming along the trail behind them. Either Auger or Mendoza was in pursuit. However, he had the lead and was in open country. Frank believed he was more resourceful than Auger or Mendoza and had an advantage as long as he kept heading to the high ground.

Watching the chase teams along the jungle path behind him, Frank didn't believe they knew exactly where they were going. These men had to be Auger's local tough guys, the ones more likely to run off in a fight. The musclemen brought by Mendoza were better trained for a fight and a lot more organized.

Frank and Cheryl arrived at the abandoned shacks of the logging camp, which had been shut down years ago. It was quiet and peaceful. Inside one of the shacks Frank turned to Cheryl. "Tell me about this disc," he demanded.

Cheryl slumped into a rickety chair and sighed. "Gary got the disc from a drug user he started to supply. The guy worked in some government office," Cheryl said. "Anyway, this guy said they could make a ton of money from some computer program that identified Coast Guard air and sea patrols in the Caribbean and up and down the coast of Central America. So Gary starts making noise with some drug dealers that he has something to sell, and then, after a while, these two guys from Costa Rica show up looking to buy the program," Cheryl explained.

Frank recognized Cheryl's story instantly for what it was, a law enforcement sting that had set its hook into Gary. He was their pigeon.

"And these guys from Costa Rica wanted a test, right?" Frank asked. Local, state or federal, all cops, and most bad guys used the same tricks of the trade.

"Yes," Cheryl said emphatically.

Frank and Cheryl rested and talked some more. The minutes wore on.

"Gary believed he was going to make one huge deal and disappear as a millionaire," Cheryl said. "The deal was set for two million dollars cash. It was to be delivered to him in half-million payments over two days in four cities. Gary chose Indianapolis, Minneapolis, Chicago and Milwaukee as the delivery cities," she continued.

Frank just listened. Gary sounded like the worst kind of amateur.

"Everyone, Gary, Patty and the Costa Ricans dealers, met in Indianapolis. At that initial meeting, Gary said he wanted more money. He said the program was worth more."

"Where did Gary get his courage?" Frank asked. "That's a pretty ballsy move for a small-time dealer to pull off."

"Gary was also a small-time user," Cheryl said.

"Great," Frank added, "He was filled with phony courage."

"I'm afraid that was true," she conceded. "Anyway, one of the Costa Ricans made a phone call. I think that's when the orders were given to kill Gary," Cheryl said. "They did it in Indianapolis."

"How exactly do you know all this?" Frank finally asked.

"Patty told me everything, and then she robbed me," Cheryl said sadly.

Recounting the story to Frank, Cheryl said, "Patty and Gary were staying in some cheap motel where they all met to get the first payment of money. When one of the Costa Ricans went outside to his car to get something, Gary followed him believing he had more money. The dealer shot him in the parking lot. The Costa Ricans all took off and left Gary dead in the parking lot. Patty snatched up the money in the motel room and took off into the night. She got the disc from Gary's hiding place in a park near the motel, came home to my house in Minnesota, and told me everything. I went to the kitchen to get her something to eat. That's when she stole my passport and credit cards and ran off. I had an idea she was coming here and I knew, or I believed, I could get in and out of Costa Rica through the abused women's underground. At that time I trusted the man I knew as Father Blanco," Cheryl said.

"Patty came here believing she might still get a deal from these people," Cheryl added. "How stupid was that?"

"Very stupid," Frank agreed.

"When I got down here, I found Patty with the help of the women's underground. It wasn't hard. American women alone who aren't tourists stand out down here. I tried to talk her out of going through with her plan. I told her it was too dangerous, only she had already made contact with someone who claimed to have a connection to Mendoza. I left in anger. When I returned, the police had swarmed down on her hotel. I heard them speaking to people in the halls. I knew it had to involve Patty, so I ran. She had told me earlier where she had hidden her cash and the disc in case something happened, which it did. So I took everything and I've been running ever since."

"Does any of this make sense to you?" Cheryl asked.

"Yes," Frank sighed. "Actually, it makes too much sense," he said. "The disc is a phony," Frank said.

"What?" she said.

"It's a fake. Gary and his friends managed to steal the disc because someone wanted them to steal it and get it into Mendoza's hands. It's a Trojan horse. Some intelligence team planned to use the disc to draw Mendoza or someone else into their snare," he said.

"I can't believe that," Cheryl said.

"Believe it. There is a U.S. military team down here tracking these guys. If the disc were real, why wouldn't the feds just shut down the network? No, for their plan to work and for us to get out alive, we have to behave as if this disc is the real McCoy. If Mendoza suspects it's a fake, we get killed, and he disappears. It's that simple," he said.

Frank didn't want to tell her what she probably suspected, that she, and then Frank, were the next links in the chain. Mendoza had to deal with loose ends, no matter what else happened.

It was clear now to Frank that Greco's team planned to capture Mendoza somewhere along the route he used to move his drugs into the United States. Aiken's guys in Washington probably planned to feed phony information about drug interdiction teams into the fake network they set up. Mendoza, acting on the information, would be moved right into Greco's trap on the ground.

Their plan, however, became unglued when Cheryl arrived looking for Patty. The local cops were drawn into a murder investigation of a woman they believed was Cheryl. Only Cheryl wasn't the victim, it was Patty who was dead. When Frank called his contact in Washington, who in turned called the embassy, it only stirred the pot more. Too many people in dark places were being dragged into the light as this scheme unraveled. Frank knew that Greco and his boss were trying to regain control of the operation, and fast.

Cheryl and Frank rested. He assessed everything she told him. Neither one heard the movement outside the logging camp's shack. They were too tired. Suddenly, Kenny kicked open the door to the shack and pointed an automatic pistol at Frank.

"Freeze!" he commanded.

Kenny looked around feverishly. "Where's the dog?" he asked.

"I don't know," Frank said. "He's kind of a free spirit. He just took off."

"I don't believe you. Get the dog and tie him up, or I put a bullet in the woman," Kenny said, turning the pistol toward Cheryl. "Want to test me?"

Frank froze. Kenny looked at him and took aim at Cheryl with the revolver.

"OK, OK," Frank said. "Dutch, come on boy," he called. The dog walked out of the shadows to his side. Frank slipped a rope around Dutch's neck and tied him to a post in the room.

"Good move," Kenny said.

Frank slowly slid his hand behind his back for the handle of the commando knife wedged in his belt.

"Easy," Kenny said. "Just slide that knife over here. You know what they say, never bring a knife to a gunfight."

Frank stood still. He withdrew the knife and scabbard from his belt and slid them across the floor toward Kenny.

"I thought you'd be long gone by now," Frank said to Kenny. "I mean, Mendoza tossed you overboard and the local cops will be at the farm pretty soon. What's left for you?" Frank asked.

"My notebook, I want my notebook," Kenny said. "My men will be here shortly. They move too slowly for me. I came ahead to get my property and take care of you two. The two of you ruined a sweet deal for me, the best deal I ever had. I was set for life, but I can still salvage some of it. After I take care of you, I can create a new set-up for myself, maybe even a better one."

Frank eyed the notebook among other things on the table. "You think you can blackmail the people in the book and use the cash to re-establish yourself somewhere else," Frank chuckled. "Do you have any idea what kind of people you're dealing with? You should put that cassock back on and thank God Mendoza didn't kill you on the spot earlier today. Believe me, the people in your book won't hesitate for a second to get rid of you," Frank said. "If you try and squeeze those people, *Padre*, you're going to learn real fast what dust-to-dust really means."

"I disagree. You're just a dumb street cop. I've come to learn that prominent people detest bad publicity," Kenny said.

"You're delusional, Kenny," Frank replied.

"I don't think so. I've watched Mendoza make people squirm. It's pretty easy when you have something to hang over their heads," Kenny said.

Frank just shook his head. He was incredulous that Kenny was so naïve. "You're in over your head, Kenny. And where are your boys? Think this through," Frank said. "It's not going to end well for you."

Glancing over at Cheryl, Frank saw a strange look in her eye.

"You enjoyed sending those women into slavery," she said calmly to Kenny.

"It was business, and I would have put your friend on the market, too, except she was a crazy bitch. I had to take her out of the picture," Kenny revealed. "My boys are coming, too," he said to Frank, "Don't worry about them. I just don't need them right now. I have everything under control."

Frank shook his head. "Kenny, you're in the deep end of the pool."

"Shut up," he shot back.

"You killed Patty?" Cheryl asked, ignoring the back and forth with Frank.

"Yes, I was saving that tidbit of information for Mendoza. I thought he'd appreciate my efforts. He may come around and appreciate me yet when he finds out I killed the two of you," Kenny said.

"Frank," Cheryl asked, "Do you have his notebook, the one with the information detailing where and to whom he sold the women?"

"Yes," Frank said.

"Yeah, the book. Give me the book," Kenny demanded as he swung around, cocking and pointing the revolver at Frank.

With the sound of the hammer locking into place as Kenny turned the gun toward Frank, Cheryl reached into the duffle bag that she had taken from the main house. She pulled out another gun. Kenny swung back around to take aim at her. She fired immediately and shot him in the chest. Kenny slumped to the ground dead.

Cheryl stood there watching the life drain from his body. She was motionless, her body frozen in place.

"What have I done?" she whimpered.

Frank tried to clear the ringing in his ears from the gunshot and listen for anyone else who might be approaching. "Let's go," he finally said. "That shot will bring his friends."

Gathering up their gear and untying Dutch, they fled from the logging shack into the jungle again.

Fifteen

When he wasn't on the water, Frank preferred the high ground of Costa Rica. The two locations offered him the greatest freedom and protection. He always felt uncomfortable anyplace where he might be surrounded or cornered. High in the mountains he was safe until he could find a way back to the *Celtic Mistress.* Being on the run as he was now made him more aware of his safe havens. There was still a group following him, and it was an issue that had to be addressed sooner rather than later. From a distance, they appeared disorganized and slow. That worked to his advantage. Unfortunately, Costa Rica was their country, and that worked to his disadvantage.

"You haven't said anything about what happened back there," Cheryl said.

"Where?" he asked.

"Don't be coy. Back there in the shack with Kenny," she said.

"Kenny's dead, and the world is better place with him gone."

"But I killed a man."

"He would have killed us," Frank said, "and I killed that guy at the farm."

"Is killing that easy for you, Frank? You were a much gentler person when we were younger. What happened to you?" she asked.

"We're in a high stakes battle. Do you want to survive?" Frank shot back. "I guarantee you the guys chasing us plan to survive. And they are not worrying about the cost in lives, either. They will do what they have to do to survive and win, just as we have to."

"This whole mess has been a trail of death, starting with Gary and Patty," Cheryl lamented. "I killed a man over a fake computer program."

"You killed a man who victimized women at their weakest moment. Those women he sold on the black market came to him for help. He violated their trust. You didn't start this mess. Mendoza and Auger had blood on their hands long before they came across us. Gary, Patty, you, me or anyone else mixed up in this would be expendable to these kinds of people. It's the way they live," Frank said.

"Apparently, it's the way you live, too," she said. "You haven't shown any remorse."

"This isn't the time for that conversation, Cheryl," he said. She was still clutching the bag she grabbed from the farmhouse. "Let me see that," he demanded.

Inside the duffle bag were three short stock assault weapons, a handful of ammunition clips and three revolvers. "Why did you take this bag?" Frank asked.

"I don't know why, instinct maybe," Cheryl replied. "Father Blanco always had this bag close by every time I saw him. I figured it was worth something. It was open, and I saw the handgun when we broke into the shack. Something just came over me when I heard him talk about selling the girls and killing Patty," she said.

"We might just get out of this alive," Frank said. "We need to get to the next ridge. Those guys are getting closer."

As the day wore on, Frank and Cheryl climbed higher and higher into the hills. Every time Frank looked back, Auger's men were still following.

"I know what you're thinking," Cheryl said. "You are trying to concoct a plan where you'll hunt them like animals and kill them. Isn't there some other way out of this without killing those men?" she asked.

He looked at her and then down the hill at the men still advancing through the jungle. She was right. Up to this moment, Frank had only thought of overpowering them and taking their lives first in order to survive.

"They'll kill us if they get the chance," Frank said. "You killed their boss."

"Please, Frank. There has to be at least one other option. All I ask is that you try and think of another way. Then do what has to be done. Can you do this for me?"

"There are caves over on the next hill," he told Cheryl. "If we can make it over there without leaving a trail, maybe we can shake these guys and just let them stumble around in the jungle. They're Kenny's thugs. They won't be as capable of catching us as Mendoza's guys might be," he said.

Cheryl smiled. "Thank you," she said. She couldn't ask for more. He was trying.

During the next several hours Frank, Cheryl and Dutch started wending their way down one hill and up and over the next hill. Using a series of hand signals, stopping often to hide, they found themselves watching Auger's men climbing up through the hills as they descended. The hike took more time than an assault, but it was what Cheryl wanted, and the plan was working.

Frank and Cheryl managed to avoid Auger's men completely. They arrived at the bottom of a hill and launched an ascent up another hill, up to the protection of the caves ahead. Without Kenny pressing them on or promising big rewards, the men might simply give up, Frank thought.

Or maybe not.

They were tired, but the climb up the second hill seemed easier now that they were no longer being chased. They began to relax. Frank found a cave that gave him the strategic advantage of a clear sight line down the hill. He was able to see anyone approaching. The position also offered an escape route.

"What now?" Cheryl asked as she settled down in the mouth of the cave just out of the sun. Inside the cave it was cool in contrast to the blazing jungle heat outside. Frank and Cheryl's stress levels dropped.

"Now we rest. We have to figure out how to get to the *Celtic Mistress*," Frank said, sliding to the ground against the cool stone wall. After a few moments, he hustled them deeper into the cave. He stopped at a point where the light from the cave's opening faded. Farther down, everything was just a black hole of darkness, much like the situation, Frank thought. The atmosphere in the cave changed from cool to damp the deeper they went into it. All the same, it was a perfect place to hide, at least for now.

The pathways heading into the dark were muddy and slippery. Frank didn't relish escaping into the cave's depth.

"What about Eddie and Connie?" Cheryl asked. "How do you think they are making out?"

"I suspect they're having a rough time. There was gunfire back there; someone was in a shootout," Frank said.

Cheryl said nothing. She stared at Frank and tried to see the young man she knew from beach parties along the Connecticut shore. Instead, she found herself looking at a man hardened beyond his years and full of anger.

"You've been through a lot," she said, "more than just this mess, I can tell," Cheryl said. "Want to talk about it?"

"Me? I'm just a retired cop still hooked on chasing bad guys," he joked.

"No, there's more," she said. "You've been hurt, and the wound is still open. I see it all the time in the women I deal with at the shelter. They all thought their lives were perfect until the husband, boyfriend, whatever, turned into a violent, cruel animal. Ultimately, the men take all their anger out on them. Most of the women take it because they can't believe what's happening and they don't know what to do about it," she said. "Their lives, the lives they knew, disappear, and they are locked in a struggle with a stranger in the body of the man they once loved. Strangely enough, many of them still love the guy, despite the changes. I don't understand all of it; every case is different. I have only dealt with the broken pieces," Cheryl said.

"Look at you, violence is a way of life. You live alone in a foreign country, and your best friend is a wild dog nobody else can get near or touch. There was a radical change somewhere in your life. What happened to you?" she asked again.

Frank sat and poked at the ground with a stick. He looked at Dutch resting at his feet and realized that with his free hand, he was unconsciously stroking the animal's ear. Finally he looked up and said, "The bottom fell out from under me all at once. Disaster struck with the force of a hurricane and ravaged my entire life. In short, my wife, who was everything to me, was killed by a madman, and he's still out there, somewhere."

"Listening is what I do best," Cheryl offered. "Want to talk about it?"

"I haven't really talked to anyone about it for a long time," Frank said.

"Might be time to start."

And so he did. For the next two hours Frank spoke without stopping about how he and Susan were shot by the same madman. Frank kept talking and talking. Somehow, Cheryl had hit a nerve, and there was no stopping him. Everything came spewing out in a seemingly endless stream.

"She was my life," Frank said.

Cheryl said nothing. She just listened, as she had for hundreds of others.

"Why am I doing this?" Frank asked. "We're being chased by people who probably want to kill us, and I'm sitting here talking about history. This won't get us to safety."

"That depends on how you define safety," she said, ignoring their situation. "You need to have a better understanding of who and what you are today if you want to help others. Through this whole mess you haven't thought of yourself once, only other people," Cheryl said. "Everything you have done has been for the benefit of someone else, even taking care of Dutch. You saved his life, too."

"You think there are many people who care about me?" he asked.

"I think there are probably more people who care about you than you might realize," she told Frank.

"Name one," he challenged.

"Eddie," she said. "I've watched the two of you. He thinks of you as a friend. He may have had his own motives for getting involved, but has there been one moment when he wasn't on your side? Don't mess that up," she advised. "Good friends are hard to come by, and we generally find them in unusual places and at strange times."

Frank smiled at the thought he had a friend. Eddie had been loyal to him during this mess. That was true, and Frank knew he had been hard on him at times.

"So, what's happened in your life?" Frank asked. "Like you said, it's been a lot of years. How did you get hooked up in this runaway project?"

Fair was fair, Cheryl thought. He was bound to ask about her life. She prepared herself as he spoke. Cheryl had faced the question before, and no matter how much time had passed, it still made her uneasy. Her own therapist often said facing her past might always be difficult. People take varying lengths of time to heal, and many never forget their personal trauma. She decided simply to be straightforward with Frank.

"I was an abused wife."

"You?" Frank said with disbelief.

"Yes. It began when my husband started to have problems at work. Eventually he was fired and never recovered emotionally. He started to take his frustrations out on me. Finally, when he broke my jaw, I got tired of telling people I fell down the stairs, so I went to the police."

Frank had never suspected anything. He sat in the cave silent, not knowing what to say.

"A detective, a guy a lot like you, went to see Sam and tell him to lay off me. That was my husband, his name was Sam. The cops warned me the case might be weak because there were no witnesses, and I didn't have any proof," she said. "Anyway," Cheryl continued, "the detective went to see Sam and told him. As the police feared, Sam denied everything. But he was stupid. He threw a punch at the cop. So Sam got busted by the detective for assaulting a police officer. After he was in custody he went into a rage and said he should have killed me," she said. "That took care of any question about him beating me," she said.

"Case closed," Frank said. "The cop got assaulted, Sam admitted to beating you, the courts convicted, right?" Frank asked optimistically.

"Right," she said, "but there's one more chapter. After he went away to jail, he got killed in prison. Wife beaters don't fare well in prison, I'm told."

Frank just shook his head.

"So where did that leave me? Sam was arrested, convicted, jailed and killed. As far as society was concerned, it was all over. Sam was caught and punished. Some might say God stepped in and punished him, too. However, in the real world I was still a wreck. I couldn't work, I was jittery all the time, and I was alone. It was a tough time until I ran into a priest who just let me talk. He was the one who challenged me to do something for someone else. 'Do a kindness, a simple kindness, for one person' he said. So I did."

Cheryl appeared emotional at times as she told her story. With the priest's help, she had committed to helping other women in need, she recalled. She took the priest's advice and started with one woman and a plan to be positive.

"Eventually, I earned a master's degree in psychology and raised money for a woman's center. From there I became involved in the underground network that helped women escape to other parts of the country and the world," she said.

"At that point, Father Blanco popped up," Frank offered.

"Yes, someone from the farm came to me and said a man he called Father Blanco had heard about my work. We started talking, and this person offered me opportunities for women in need. I had never spoken to anyone outside the underground. Yet, this person seemed to know I was involved in rescue work," Cheryl said.

"Kenny was a scummy little bastard, but he wasn't stupid. He had ways to find out things," Frank said. "He probably delivered that same pitch to others doing the kind of work you were doing. Your network was probably blended into a larger operation, a network Kenny controlled without your knowledge."

"I know of women who made it to good places," she said.

"Kenny had to do that to make it look good. There had to be success stories out there to make it easier to hide the ones who got lost in the system," Frank said.

"Well, it was the underground that brought me here. When Patty stole my passport, I knew she was headed for trouble, and the underground seemed to be the best way to follow her and help. A lot of good it did," she said. "I didn't know Father Blanco was connected to the same drug gang Gary and Patty were dealing with back home," she said. "How could I have been so stupid?"

"Don't be so hard on yourself," Frank offered. "It sounds like you did a lot of good for people in need. You're not responsible for other people's cruelty."

Cheryl told Frank about taking the disc from the flophouse where Patty was staying before she was killed. She knew where Patty hid the disc.

"What about the money Patty got in the States from the Costa Ricans?" Frank asked.

"Patty took some to cover her travel costs here and hid the rest," she said. "She took enough to live quite well down here for a while."

"Do you know where the rest of Mendoza's money is hidden?" he asked.

"Yes," she said cautiously.

"Good, don't tell anyone." he said.

The two of them looked at each other. They were no longer the same young people who summered together, picnicking on the beach. Each was struggling to rebuild a new life from the ashes of a personal disaster. Frank and Cheryl's current lives in Costa Rica converged with two sets of armed men chasing them through the jungle, and as they ran, each simply hoped there would be a tomorrow to enjoy.

Frank reached out for Cheryl and held her. She buried her face in his chest and started to cry. The steeliness of her determination to survive Sam was melting, and for the first time in a long time, despite the gunmen chasing her, she felt protected. With Frank, she believed she had hope.

Stroking her hair, Frank felt the warmth of her breath on his neck. It was the first time since Susan died that he enjoyed such a feeling of closeness. *This woman will survive,* he swore to himself. *This woman won't be taken away.* He was starting to have conflicting feelings. Was he being unfaithful to Susan? She was gone, he understood that. Would she understand his feelings for Cheryl? He held her close and simply accepted the moment. He let his mind drift back to that summer in Connecticut when they were young and carefree. It had been a long time since he had allowed himself to let his guard down and simply be himself.

Cheryl felt calm, too. Here, with danger looming, she had someone to protect her. She hadn't really trusted any man for several years. Her husband had driven that capability from her, and Kenny had proved her right in believing, until now, that many men could not be trusted. Only here with Frank, tucked away up in the hills, she felt safe. He wanted nothing from her and gave her everything. She remembered she used to believe this was the way things should be between two people. It was a sensation lost to her for a long time.

After all these years, Frank had stepped back into Cheryl's life at a time of need and danger, and he was willing to risk everything for her. It had been a long time since any man had been willing to do half that much for her. The last man in her life used her for a punching bag. Frank was a hard man, too, but he was focused on good. She believed that about him. She believed it with all her heart, and she knew believing it meant she had a chance of surviving this crisis.

Huddled in each other's arms, they drifted off to sleep. It was a quiet, restful sleep. It was also short-lived. Dutch gave off his low growl, a warning someone was approaching. The sound broke the couple's shared moments of tenderness.

"There's someone out there. Stay here," Frank ordered.

Cheryl snapped back into her defensive mode in an instant. The sense of calm that had washed over her for a brief time was gone again.

Frank slipped to the edge of the cave with an assault rifle. He flipped the safety to the off position. He expected to see Auger's men, floundering around the jungle below. He didn't see anything on the road approaching the cave, or any movement in the bush in the surrounding area. The birds were quiet and the animals were still. Dutch still growled, low and steady.

"I hear you, boy. Stay quiet," Frank whispered. He silently waved Cheryl back deeper into the cave. With his finger to his lips he signaled for her to be quiet. She moved slowly back into the cave as instructed. Whoever was out there knew the jungle better than Auger's hired thugs.

Finally, a white cloth on a stick shot up in the air from the brush and a male voice called out, "*Senor! Aqui!*"

Frank took aim on the general area of the flag and shouted back, "Show yourself! Now!"

The white flag waved in the wind for a few seconds. Finally a young man appeared from behind a boulder about fifty feet away. He stood erect with his arms extended. Frank alternated pointing his weapon at the flag and at the man, trying to decide where and whether to shoot.

"I am alone, *senor*. I came to help!" he said.

"Who the hell are you?" Frank asked.

"I am Victor. You know my father Hector," he said.

"Hector? The man at the restaurant?" Frank asked.

"*Si*, he is a friend of *Senor* Greco. I was sent to bring you back. My brother is tracking your friend and the other women."

"Frank, it's help! We're going to make it!" Cheryl shouted from inside the cave.

"Quiet," Frank ordered. Turning back to the young man, he said, "Prove to me who you are."

The youth smiled. "You took that knife on your belt from *Senor* Greco's man at my father's restaurant. You tried to return it, but *Senor* Greco said it was yours to keep."

Frank smiled. Greco had sent the boy. There was no way for a Mendoza man to know about the knife's history. Only Greco or someone he told would know what transpired at Hector's restaurant that day.

"We have people following us," he told the boy. "We must move fast."

"That is not a problem," he answered. "*Senor* Greco sent a team of men to make sure you were safe after you fled the farm. They took care of the *cocaineros* chasing you," he said calmly. "*Senor* Greco's men are regrouping now for their own escape." Frank never asked the boy what he had meant when he said Greco's men took care of the *cocaineros*. He just knew.

"You have a vehicle?" Frank asked.

"*Si, senor*, I have a truck at the bottom of the hill," he said.

Frank smiled and called to Cheryl to get their weapons. This was their chance.

Sixteen

Back at Father Blanco's farm, a gun battle raged on. Greco's team forced Mendoza's men to retreat from the airstrip back to the main compound under a heavy barrage of gunfire. The drug lord's men took up refuge in the main *hacienda* and the huts where the women and Father Blanco's disciples had lived. Blanco's religious followers had scattered to the wind and across the countryside when the shooting started.

Greco's men continued their fire-and-run attack. Over and over throughout the battle, the mercenary team repositioned themselves in the compound. Mendoza's men were well armed and good shots, but they lacked strategic talents necessary to be effective in full-blown field combat operations. The *cocainero* soldiers were more comfortable simply laying down a heavy cover of gunfire and overpowering a weaker, disorganized opposition force. Greco's fighting style didn't give them a main position to overrun. He kept moving his men like chess pieces.

Greco himself kept changing his position, all the while staying in radio contact with his men and allowing him to run the show. The tactic confused his opponents and denied them the ability to organize any type of useful offensive against an identifiable target. While the gun battle raged on, amid the smoke a single Land Rover SUV slowly inched its way toward the crop field and disappeared down a dirt road.

"This is team leader. Status reports," Greco screamed into his radio.

"Opposition scattered around the compound," the first squad leader reported. "These guys have no idea what to do next."

"They appear to have lost their commanders," the second squad leader radioed to the team. "They are completely confused."

"Status report on the friendlies," Greco demanded.

"All got away. They made it into the bush as expected. Be advised, one small opposition team took off after Reardon and an unidentified woman. No one was observed following the other group," the first squad leader answered.

"Sting the opposition again," Greco said. "Reardon will take care of himself. Send two men to pick up his trail. Make sure he meets up with the intercept. Have our people provide support as necessary. Afterwards, instruct our team members to proceed to the designated rendezvous point. I'm calling in a wrap-up strike and extraction team. We're getting out of here," Greco said.

"Already done," a voice came back.

With no leaders, the opposition still managed to return heavy fire. They had no intention of surrendering. Their opposition would be short-lived, however.

Greco called in for his air support and ordered all his men to retreat from the compound and take cover along the far side of the crop field. In a few minutes a Sikorsky Blackhawk MH 60-K appeared from the south over the treetops and assumed a prominent presence in the sky over the farm.

The Blackhawk helicopter circled the compound. On Greco's command a continuous stream of bullets fired from the chopper's machine guns and tore into the main house and huts of Father Blanco's farm. In a relentless barrage of firepower, walls were ripped to shreds and beams that kept the huts raised off the ground were sliced, causing the buildings to collapse under their own weight. The Blackhawk fired rockets into the main house and several rooms burst into a blaze. After the main attack, the helicopter circled the compound and fired continuously. The air attack went on non-stop for about fifteen minutes. After the first five minutes all return fire had ended.

Greco radioed to the chopper to hover until his team checked out the grounds. Nothing moved in the wreckage of the huts or the house. None of Mendoza's men who stayed behind survived the attack. If all was going well with the plan, the "friendlies" were slowly making their way back to the *Celtic Mistress*.

The team determined Mendoza was in the SUV that had disappeared during the fight. The drug dealer's body wasn't found anywhere in the compound. What that meant for Reardon and his people was unclear. All Greco was able to do was relay the information to Aikens.

In Limon, Aikens paced the terrace of his hotel room, waiting for updates from the field. His phone rang, and he answered it on the first ring.

"Mr. Aikens, I am Frank Reardon's friend in Washington. We've never formally met. However, I believe you are aware of me," said a voice known to every intelligence and security boss in the country.

"What can I do for you?" Aikens asked politely. He didn't ask the man how he acquired his private cell phone number. It would have been a stupid question.

"You are in the midst of a mission, Mr. Aikens. I realize you inherited a mess from another agency and have worked hard to resolve it. However, I fear I need to complicate it a bit more," the voice said.

"I'm listening," Aikens said respectfully.

"How are you getting Reardon and those people out of Costa Rica while protecting them from the Mendozas of the world?" the voice asked.

Aikens explained his plan for everyone to meet at the *Celtic Mistress* and sail to a beach south of Limon for a nighttime helicopter extraction. Greco and his men had another escape route over land. Everyone was headed to a friendly neighboring country.

"Negative. For many reasons I can't explain here, we must not have any more incursions onto foreign soil regarding this mission. You will need to bring Captain Ruiz into the fold. He can help. He is being briefed as we speak. He will be cooperative. This is how I will help you," the voice said, explaining the details of a new plan of action. After a detailed outline of the plan and a description of other assets being made available, the voice asked, "Any questions?"

"What about my field team?" Aikens asked, aware he was unable to debate the new plan.

"Let them proceed as planned. With any luck, their talents will keep them under the radar," the voice said.

"Can I ask a question, one not related to the mission?" Aikens replied.

There was a pause on the line. Finally, the man said, "I suppose you're entitled."

"Why? Why the constant support for Reardon? What's the deal with him? He's just a local cop," Aikens said.

"Loyalty, Mr. Aikens. You should understand that. What you really want to know are the circumstances that brought us together," the voice said. After a pause the man quietly said, "He gave back to me something I hold very dear."

Aikens knew nothing more was going to be offered. The cryptic explanation was all he was going to get. However, Aikens understood. There was a trust between this man and Reardon, in the same way he and Greco trusted each other.

"I'll get the word to our people," Aikens answered.

"Good," the voice simply said before the caller disconnected.

Aikens stood on his hotel terrace with the phone in one hand and a cigar in the other. He looked out over the Limon harbor where Frank usually docked the *Celtic Mistress*, tucked away among the cargo ships and away from the cruise ships. This Reardon was a strange man, Aikens thought. In all the Caribbean, he chose to dock his boat among the rusting trawlers and weather-beaten cargo ships that hauled all sorts of materials between the islands and down to the northern ports of South America. Reardon chose this kind of port rather than a place lined with sleek, white recreational vessels that carried fun seekers as their cargo. At first he thought Reardon might be hiding from his past in this out-of-the-way dump, but now he believed the former cop was comfortable here in Limon. Aikens took a slow drag on the cigar and called

Captain Ruiz. Then he called the embassy and issued a few more orders.

As Greco's men finished their work at Blanco's farm, Eddie continued to make his way back to town. His mission now was to meet up with Frank, if he was still alive. Greco's scouts said they saw Frank get out of the house with Cheryl after Mendoza's airplane blew up. That's all he knew. He had to believe Frank was capable of surviving. He wasn't completely sure. The plan was hatched on the fly.

"Where are we going?" Connie demanded.

Eddie stopped everyone in his entourage and stood toe-to-toe with the woman. "You pushed your way into this escape, lady. You don't get to ask questions. You don't get to vote. You just get to do as you are told or strike out on your own, all alone. I have a partner out there who is missing with the woman we came to rescue. So, just shut up and follow orders. You should be good at that," he said. "Do that, and maybe, just maybe, some of us will survive." As quickly as he had stopped, he spun around and continued his forced march back to the town.

"Do as he says," Rafael said to her quietly. "Just do as he says. He has no way of knowing for sure what has happened to the others. He can get us out of here," Rafael said. "I know he can."

Connie nodded. She knew Eddie was her ticket to whatever freedom might be ahead. Now she had to go with the flow and follow the orders of a man she didn't know.

Eddie was used to moving faster on missions. Alone was best. Commando teams, while slower, were trained to focus on the mission. Traveling with civilians, Eddie thought, was nothing more than a herding operation. He had to keep them moving and focused, and all the time working to avoid the enemy. Rafael, while not trained in military operations, did follow orders.

Up front Eddie saw a teenage boy standing alongside a beat-up old pickup truck. It was as if the youth was waiting for someone. Eddie froze and just watched. The young man was on recon and seemed to like it.

Rafael turned a corner on the road, herding the women and hauling their gear. He saw Eddie hunched down looking ahead down the road. Rafael quieted down the women and found hiding places in the bushes for them. He inched up behind Eddie.

"What do you see?" he whispered.

Eddie pointed with the barrel of his rifle.

Rafael smiled. "That's Antonio, Hector's son."

"Hector's son? The guy from the restaurant?"

"*Si, senor,*" Rafael said.

Eddie approached the boy carefully. The boy waved.

"*Senor* Greco sent me to guide you back. He wants all of you to take *Senor* Reardon's boat to open water. He said you need to go to these coordinates," the boy said, handing Eddie a piece of paper.

"I don't know where *Senor* Reardon is," Eddie said.

"My brother does," the boy said with a smile.

Seventeen

The two trucks driven by Hector's sons arrived at the dock simultaneously. They circled around the waterfront until they spotted each other. No one knew how many men Mendoza had working for him, what had happened to the force at the farm, or if reinforcements were on the way. Hector didn't want the *Celtic Mistress'* passengers standing around in the open as easy targets.

Frank and Eddie jumped out of their respective trucks and hugged each other. "Everyone OK?" Frank asked.

"Rattled but in one piece. Hector's boy gave me this piece of paper. Greco wants you to take the *Celtic Mistress* to these coordinates on the open water," Eddie said.

"That is the middle of nowhere," Frank said, looking over Eddie's shoulder at the location described on the slip of paper. "How did he come up with that location?"

Eddie shrugged. "That's the plan. Either you trust these people, or we do something else," he said.

Frank sighed. "How are you fixed for weapons?"

"I have some, enough to make a stand. A short stand," Eddie said.

"Load up, get everyone on board. We're leaving now." Frank had to decide whether to leave or stay and fight. He realized he wasn't equipped to hold off Mendoza's gang. He had to run, even if it was into the unknown.

"Where are we going?" one of the women asked.

"Damned if I know," Frank said without looking around to see who raised the question.

Suddenly, rumbling could be heard. Trucks were coming. Frank turned around to Hector. Manny, the dock chief from Limon, stood behind Hector.

"I underestimated you," Frank said to Hector. "You are more than you appear, but I'm not sure exactly what you are."

"I am a friend of *Senor* Greco. That's all," he said.

"Yeah, right," Frank laughed. He withdrew the knife and scabbard from his belt.

"I took this from a man at your place; Greco told me to keep it. Your son used it to prove his identity to me in the hills."

"It's yours," Hector said.

"Maybe, but I want you to keep it," Frank said. "It'll be our bond, something that ties us together."

Hector smiled and took the knife. "Go, go now. Time is short. Some day you will come back for this," he said to Frank. "Is there anything else I can do for you?"

"Thanks," Frank said. "I need you to send a few of my personal things from Limon to Connecticut," Frank said. "It may be a while before I get back here."

"Anything," Hector said.

Frank smiled and quickly detailed his needs.

Then he spun around and called to Manny.

"What are you doing here?"

"Captain Ruiz told me to come and see that you got safely away," he said with a laugh. It was the first time Frank saw Manny show any humor.

"Ruiz sent you?"

"Yes, Ruiz sent me."

"I don't understand."

"You don't need to understand. We're here to help; it's that simple," Manny said.

The two men smiled at each other. They shook hands.

The sound of the approaching trucks grew louder. Concern swept over Frank's face.

"Did Ruiz send those guys coming in the truck?" Frank hollered as a truckload of armed men raced toward the dock.

Manny spun around. "Mendoza men! Get aboard your boat now! Leave!"

Frank, with Dutch at his heels, boarded the *Celtic Mistress* and fired up the engines. Rafael stowed their gear, made sure all the women were aboard, then jumped on himself. Eddie started a weapons check. The boat pulled away from the dock slowly, cleared the small harbor, and sped away.

As he left the dock Frank heard gunfire. He turned and saw Hector's sons firing rifles at the men on the truck. Manny crouched in the center of the dock in a combat position, firing his 5.7mm pistol. Frank saw him eject a clip, rapidly insert another twenty-shot clip, and continue firing. The sound of gunfire was lost in the air as the *Celtic Mistress* roared away.

Frank headed east out into the Caribbean Sea as instructed, not knowing what awaited him. At sea he and Eddie spotted a speedboat rushing up the coastline from the south. It was charging toward them on an intercept course. Moments later, a second speedboat appeared on the horizon and joined the first vessel in the chase.

"It's Mendoza's navy," Eddie yelled to Frank.

"We can't outrun those guys. Those speedboats will be on top of us soon," Frank yelled. He pressed the throttle all the way forward, pushing his boat faster and faster into the wind. The rpms of the engine rose to their highest levels. He still didn't know where he was going or what awaited him out on the water. All he could do was have faith in the people around him. The loss of control made him uneasy, but he pressed on.

Frank had read enough DEA advisories while on the police force to know drug dealers in Central America added lightweight speedboats to their assortment of tools to move drugs up the coastline. Equipped with high speed engines, the boats plied the shallow coastal waters out of reach of Coast Guard cutters and were too small to attract the attention of air patrols. Mendoza, too, saw value to the speedboats. He tweaked their use to make them part of his weapons arsenal, as well. He outfitted a handful of the so-called "go-fast" boats with high-powered deck guns.

"Keep going," Eddie said. "Head out to blue water," he commanded while scanning the sea and sky. Every boat captain knew blue water was the area where fishermen found the biggest catch. Frank feared he was becoming the fish in this battle.

The engines groaned as they propelled the fishing boat farther out to open sea. The Celtic Mistress cut through the water and bounced on the waves as Mendoza's men in the speedboats continued to close the gap on Frank's boat. Frank knew his lead was evaporating with each passing second.

"Where are we going?" Frank yelled. "What's out here?"

"Just trust me," Eddie said. "You need to trust me."

Frank nodded and kept the engines at full power. He looked out onto the water ahead of him and saw only sea and sky. Other than surrendering, all he could do was keep the power on and press forward, even as the speedboats continued to give chase. Frank had come to trust Eddie. Why, he didn't know, but he had grown to accept the former jungle fighter as an ally in this misadventure.

"How did you get my security code, the one I use to call my D.C. friend, the code Cheryl whispered in my ear at the farm?" Frank asked.

"It was Aikens. I think he's figured out the identity of your secret buddy. And don't look at me. I don't know who he is. Greco told me to use the code to get you to believe there was a plan."

"What is the plan now?"

"Well, it didn't include these speedboats, I can tell you that much," Eddie said. "Just keep those engines roaring."

The two men stood at the controls of the *Celtic Mistress* with the wind and sea spray in their faces, trying to coax more speed out of the engines. Deep inside, each man hoped their prayers were enough. Mendoza's boats were gaining on them.

Finally, Frank had to ask.

"How long have you known?"

"Known what?" Eddie answered.

"Not now, not here. Stop avoiding my question," Frank said. "How long have you known the disc was a fake? I want to know."

Eddie never took his eyes off the sea before him. Quietly, but loud enough for Frank to hear, he said, "I've always known. I was their guy on the ground monitoring things. I was in place fully expecting that idiot Gary to show up. Then his girlfriend arrived and got herself killed before you were drawn into the mess."

Frank pressed forward. As the boat bounced against the tide at high speeds, a crewman on one of the speedboats brought a rocket-propelled grenade launcher to his shoulder and took aim at the Celtic Mistress. Frank saw the man with the weapon and told Eddie to fire at him with an automatic rifle. The boats were about 100 yards apart now and the distance was closing.

"That won't do much," Eddie said.

"It might distract him. Maybe we'll get lucky." Frank said.

Frank and Eddie took turns in the stern firing a rifle at the guy with the rocket launcher. Mendoza's man slowed for a few seconds but regained his focus and brought his weapon to his shoulder again.

Aboard the Trident Class submarine *SSBN Long Island*, a group of civilians huddled around the communications desk and watched a scene unfold on the waters above. Radar screens and television monitors with feeds from the antennae popping up through the water showed two speedboats in hot pursuit of a fishing boat trying to make its way out into the Caribbean Sea.

Once considered the darlings of the Cold War, some of the nuclear-powered Tridents had been reconfigured to support special operations forces and their missions around the globe. Frank's high ranking Washington friend in the intelligence world had arranged for Aikens and Captain Ruiz to be jetted off for a rendezvous with the submarine. It was only within the past few hours that Aikens learned why Ruiz was part of the plan.

"*Senor* Aikens, can you direct one of these sailors to give me access to a frequency?" the police captain asked on the bridge of the submarine.

"Commander, please give our guest access to whatever he requests. I have the security clearance necessary to approve the request," Aikens said, displaying his credentials to the submarine commander.

"Sailor, surrender your headset and dial up the frequency requested by our guest," the sub commander ordered.

"Aye, aye sir," the young sailor said, unaware of what was about to happen as he handed over the equipment.

"You speak Spanish, sailor?" the commander asked quietly.

"Fluently, sir," the submariner answered.

"Translate everything he says as things proceed. Understand?"

"Completely sir," the sailor said.

On the open water, Frank decided it was time to abandon ship. He knew the end was very near for the *Celtic Mistress*, and he had no idea what was in the future.

"Jump, everyone off, now," Frank screamed. He looked at Dutch and pushed him in the water, unsure if he'd ever see him again.

One by one the group jumped off the port side of the boat, out of sight of the oncoming speedboats bearing down on the starboard side of the *Celtic Mistress*. The shooter with the rocket-propelled grenade launcher peered through his scope at the *Celtic Mistress*. He was unable to see the gang on Frank's boat slipping over the side. Those few moments of gunfire confusion had slowed his attack. While he lined up Frank's boat in his sights, Eddie heard something in the sky above.

"Hear that?" Eddie screamed at Frank as everyone swam away from the *Celtic Mistress*.

Frank never had a chance to respond. His fishing boat exploded in a ball of fire behind him. All other sounds were drowned out as the gasoline tanks exploded and pieces of rubble rained down from the sky. Everyone started to grab onto a piece of floating debris. Eddie tried to remain still in the water.

"It's still there," Eddie screamed over the roar of Mendoza's speedboats still racing down on them to make a body count.

"What are you babbling about?" Frank screamed as he bobbed in the water.

"Jet engines. I hear jets!" he said.

Before the jets reached their target, a second blast from the RPG hit the water and everyone was tossed about in the tidal surge from the explosion.

Screeching down out of the clouds and flying low and fast over the water came two MiG-23s with Cuban markings. The wings on the Soviet-built jets were partially swept back. They flew side by side and were coming up behind the drug runners' speedboats. The planes roared over the speedboats. Then the Soviet jets, a gift to the Cubans, climbed into the sky and did a barrel roll. While inverted, the pilots dropped the noses of their aircraft, effecting a 180-degree turn to come racing back toward the speedboats. Lights on the consoles of both jets lit up, signifying the speedboats had been targeted by the weapons systems on the aircraft.

The police captain aboard the Trident accepted the headset and instructed the submarine's radio officer to connect him to a designated frequency. He started to speak into the microphone. "Cuban Strike Team, this is Captain Ruiz. You are aware of my authority?"

"*Si, senor,*" a voice crackled back in Spanish.

"What is your status, Cuban Strike Team?"

"We are bearing down on two speedboats. They have attacked and destroyed a fishing vessel, *senor*. We have them targeted," the senior pilot reported.

"Retaliate immediately," the captain ordered.

"*Si, senor,*" the pilot said.

"He's speaking to two Cuban MiG fighters," the radioman on the sub said to the sub commander. "They've just painted the speedboats. He's given an order for the MiGs to attack the speedboats."

All eyes turned to a video monitor above the bridge.

Machine guns on the decks of the speedboats started firing. The MiGs responded with cannon fire as they closed in on their targets. The men on the speedboats jumped into the water. In unison, the MiGs let loose with rocket fire. Two rockets hit each speedboat, which then burst into flames. Machine gun fire from the jets swept over the wreckage of the speedboats, killing all onboard. The fighter jets raced through the cloud of smoke, shot upward into the sky, and disappeared from sight.

"Targets destroyed," one pilot reported over the radio as the jets vanished from the area.

Turning to the sub commander, the police captain said, "Our country does not have the air power of Cuba. However, we have a relationship with the Cubans. In exchange for landing rights and refueling opportunities in Costa Rica, we have, well, assets, I believe you would say."

"Politics was never my strong point," the sub commander said. "Surface immediately and pick up those people from the fishing vessel, now." he ordered his crew.

In the water above, everyone from the *Celtic Mistress* felt another wave developing in the water below them. Frank was bobbing up and down in the water as the five-hundred-and-sixty-foot long *SSBN Long Island* broke the waters of the Caribbean. A hatch on the conning tower of the submarine opened and a handful of men emerged onto the observation deck with binoculars. Other hatches opened, and men in wetsuits spewed out, jumped into Zodiacs, and headed out to pick up the gang from the *Celtic Mistress.*

A Navy SEAL diver dragged Frank and Dutch into the inflatable Zodiac and wrapped them both in blankets. Exhausted but alive, Frank looked out over the water and saw the scattered wreckage of his boat. Reduced to trash, parts slowly sank to the bottom of the sea. Other parts were flushed into the current of the Caribbean waters. He shook his head, looked over the waves and spotted Cheryl in another Zodiac. He wondered if she was right when she had asked him in the hills if this mess could have been handled in another way. The fleet of Zodiacs headed back to the submarine. With the rhythmic bouncing of the raft against the waves, Frank passed out from exhaustion.

Frank woke up on a couch in the officers' mess aboard the *SSBN Long Island,* listening to the radio chatter from the bridge. The bridge crew was wrapping up the operation and preparing to submerge and leave the waters off Costa Rica for a port unknown, at least to him.

"Everyone is aboard, bridge. We're preparing to close the hatch for dive," a Navy SEAL team member said over the radio from the deck.

"Confirmed, rescue chief. Lock the hatch and confirm. We have three women, two men and a dog on board," the bridge officer said.

Two men? We're missing someone, Frank said to himself. Who was missing? Was it Eddie or Rafael? He jumped to his feet, looking for a phone. Seeing none, he headed for the door to the corridor outside.

"Excuse me, sir. You have to stay here while we submerge," a petty officer on security detail told Frank.

"No, we're missing someone. Let me by. I have to get to the bridge," Frank insisted.

"Not possible, sir. At least not right now," he said.

The guard was polite but determined. The petty officer had his orders. This was a naval vessel.

"Please get word to the captain. I want, no, I need to speak to him immediately," Frank asked. "Please do that for me?"

"As soon as I can, sir," the petty officer said, ushering Frank back inside and locking the door.

That was the end of it. Frank had to wait, a captive on a ship from his own country, until others were ready to speak to him. Even the women were segregated away from him in another area. And where was Dutch? The radio said he was onboard, but where?

On the bridge, as the *Long Island* submerged, Aikens turned to the sub captain. "What will your log say about this incident?"

"Mr. Aikens, this submarine is charged with performing covert duties. I saw a fishing boat in trouble in the Caribbean Sea. It exploded, and I rescued the passengers."

"Perfect," Aikens said.

The *Long Island* quietly submerged with no official reports filed anywhere about the Cubans and the attack on the go-fast boats. Aikens handled the submarine commander and his log with his usual efficiency. Now he had to handle Frank and the others from the *Celtic Mistress*. It had to appear as if none of them were ever aboard. Aikens made his way down to the officers' mess where Frank was waiting, desperate to know who was missing.

"What's going on?" Frank demanded to know. "And who are you?" he added, noting the man wasn't wearing a uniform.

"Easy, Reardon. My name is Thomas Aikens. In a nutshell, I'm Greco's boss," he said.

"A spook. I should have figured. Who's missing? Which one of my people didn't make it aboard?"

"Your people?"

"That was my boat that got blown to hell out there. Everyone on board was my responsibility. So yeah, they are my people," Frank shot back.

"Fair enough. Eddie is not aboard," he said.

"Eddie?" Frank asked. "Eddie is dead?"

"I'm sorry."

Frank looked at Aikens and said, "Wait a minute, Eddie was your friend. You're the guy who negotiated his release, right? Where exactly did you rescue him from?"

Aikens smiled. "That's true. I did rescue him from some backwater. Where isn't important now. I felt we owed it to him for the service he performed."

Frank slumped down on the couch and was overwhelmed by a sense of loneliness. A man he barely knew, his new friend, was gone.

"We should talk," Aikens said.

"Later," Frank answered. "I'm not in the mood right now."

Aikens took the cue. He needed Frank and his cooperation.

"OK, later then," Aikens said quietly. "We'll talk later."

Frank said nothing.

Eighteen

Submerged and heading east, away from the Central American coastline, the submarine *SSBN Long Island* left in its wake the flaming hulls of two speedboats and the *Celtic Mistress*. Within an hour there would be no trace of the three craft or the brief sea battle that sank them. The course home set for the *Long Island* was slow and circuitous through the Caribbean Sea. It took the sub out to the Atlantic and up the Eastern Seaboard. Running submerged allowed the vessel to maintain secrecy as it passed through the waters in and around the independent island nations of the Caribbean and the ever-present armada of glistening white cruise ships.

Captain Martin William Donaldson did allow the sub to surface at sunrise, providing the waters and traditional airline pathways above were clear. An hour on the surface gave his bridge officers time to get a quick breath of fresh air and helped to keep them alert.

The sub captain was a pragmatic man, a proud product of his midwestern roots. After graduation from the U.S. Naval Academy, he immediately applied for submarine duty. He believed in God and country and wanted to do his best for both. He made several secret cruises under the ice cap of the North Pole before attending the Naval War College, where he studied sea tactics and was assigned to Mission Readiness Command in Guam before getting his own boat.

In the calmness of the moment now, Donaldson felt a sense of irony while the *Long Island* passed Cuba. He passed it submerged today, despite the fact he had just partnered with the Communist country's air command in a mission. For decades the two nations had stared each other down in a geopolitical game of chicken, each waiting for the other to blink. The world would never know that the two military forces had just worked together to overcome a common enemy. *The politics of the day would never allow that kind of honesty*, he thought.

No matter, the submarine captain had successfully completed his mission. The political games of Washington were Aiken's problem. He just had to focus on bringing his boat and passengers back to Naval Submarine Base New London in Connecticut.

He knew that before anyone gave any consideration to leave for the crew, he had to get these civilians off the submarine and delivered to New London. That meant dealing with Aikens. He had intelligence people aboard on previous cruises. No matter how often he dealt with them, they always made him nervous. Intelligence people simply didn't think like military people.

Down in the dining hall, Frank was morose. Eddie was dead, and he blamed himself. He felt a cop's loss of a partner in the middle of a case. That was one of the worst things that can happen to a cop. The surviving partner usually made the call to the widow. Their partnership, however, was so new that Frank had never learned much about Eddie's personal life.

While Frank was mourning at a table, Aikens came bounding back into the room full of smiles. He sat down across from Frank with a cup of coffee and said everyone would be home soon. Aikens explained he needed to get everybody back to the U.S. undetected, hence the use of the submarine for the return trip. Rafael was a wrinkle yet to be addressed. He was sure, however, he could get him situated somewhere in the U.S. Bringing him to the States was the only way to protect him from Mendoza, who was still unaccounted for in the aftermath of the shootout at the farm. But he had to be careful. Mendoza had friends in the U.S., and Raphael had a big mouth, dangerous factors for someone who might have to live under a new identity.

"Everyone gets home except Eddie," Frank reminded him.

Aikens pushed his coffee aside. He liked the way Reardon handled himself. He thought he might want to bring him in as a field agent. He was a little older than the typical agent. Still, there might be a role for a guy with his resourcefulness in his organization. Greco had warmed to him, as Aikens had expected. Unfortunately, this wasn't the moment to bring up a job offer. *Maybe another time*, Aikens thought to himself. *Now is the time to give him some room.*

A few mornings later Aikens found Frank in the same state in the same dining area. Despite Frank's sour mood, the intelligence chief came to share some news with him.

"Good news, Mendoza is dead."

"Really? How?" Frank asked.

"Tell me, what color was the suit Mendoza wore the last time you saw him?" Aikens asked.

"Olive, nice cut as I remember, but I wasn't in the best shape for any sartorial assessments," said Frank.

"Well, Greco's team observed an SUV escaping the battle at Auger's farm," Aikens explained. "Later, on their way to their extraction point, they found it crashed in the jungle. Greco found a man shot through the heart, dead, in an olive Armani suit. It was Mendoza. Greco cut a patch of the blood-stained suit and had it expressed to D.C. for analysis. A DNA test identified the blood as Mendoza's."

"So it's over?" Frank asked with a bit more interest.

"Cut off the head of the snake, and things die out. Unfortunately, someone else will probably assume his throne down the road. It might be a while, though. In the short term, the players will fight among themselves for control, weaken the structure, and at some point get reorganized."

"I guess so," Frank said. "Life goes on, right?"

Frank found Cheryl later in the day. He appreciated that Aikens had shared the news with him about Mendoza. However, Eddie was still dead. Frank missed him. He had to put that aside, at least for a while. He needed to share the news about Mendoza with Cheryl. It might make her happy. To his surprise, she seemed unaffected.

"How do you do it?" Cheryl asked quietly.

"Do what?" Frank responded.

"How do you live in this world of killers?"

"I didn't choose it," he answered, not comfortable with where the conversation was heading.

"Yes, you did, you chose to become a cop."

"I became a cop to help people. I didn't create the bad people in the world. I just decided to help people who needed help. Sometimes you have to fight fire with fire."

"Do you enjoy it?"

"After what I've lost, you can ask that question? I've paid a price, a very high price," he said. "To be honest, though, I have mixed feelings. I didn't enjoy being a cop when Susan died. I felt helpless. I did enjoy being a cop at other times, like when I reunited a kid with his mother who had been snatched up by his crack-head father. That day is in my top ten," he said adamantly. "I was there for that kid on that day."

"I'm sorry. I was out of line," Cheryl said. "You don't deserve to be judged by me."

They were silent. They just sat quietly, feeling the slow, methodical movement of the sub through the water.

Frank wasn't mad. He understood her frustration and anger. He often felt the same way. "I'd like to see you again," Frank said finally.

"I'm not sure that's a good idea right now," Cheryl answered, "at least not in the way you're thinking."

"Why not?"

Cheryl sighed. She didn't want to hurt Frank. She felt this was just the wrong time for the two of them. "Frank, we've both been through a lot," Cheryl said. "You need to come to terms with Susan's death. You're reacting to any kindness I may have shown you during some very trying times while we were in Costa Rica. We had something years ago. It just didn't last. I don't know why. Now I think you need to resolve some other issues first—for you, not someone else. You shouldn't just jump into a relationship with the first woman who smiles at you. I am sure Susan was a wonderful woman, but she's gone now. I don't say that to be cruel, it's just a fact. And you're still alive. Wouldn't she want you to have a life?"

She paused and let the words sink in to bring a focus to the conversation.

"You're a great guy, Frank," she continued. "Right now, you're hurting. I don't know if finding your wife's killer is the answer. For you, it might be. Only you can figure that out. I do know you need to acknowledge she's gone. As for me, I have to rebuild my work and my life, too. The women I helped were my family. I have to know if I am capable of going on and doing the same kind of work. I'm not ready for a man in my life, maybe someday, just not now," she said.

Frank stood and stared at her.

"Please don't be hurt. I still very much want us to be friends again. We were friends many years ago. We can be friends now, too," Cheryl said.

He smiled. "All right, I think I understand. At least I'm going to try and understand. And yes, I'd like to be friends. Maybe I just need someone to talk to from time to time," he said.

"Anytime," Cheryl said, "day or night."

"What will you do first when we get home to the States?" Frank asked.

"That's something I've wanted to speak to you about," she said.

Frank looked at her with puzzlement.

"I know I just said I couldn't deal with a relationship, at least not now, but I've been thinking about coming back to Connecticut, specifically Bridgeport."

"That's great," Frank said.

"Wait, I meant what I said. We can be friends for now. Please don't complicate this."

"OK."

"I'm thinking of re-establishing the abuse rescue network in Connecticut. I have to go back to Minnesota," Cheryl said. "It's where my work and life were based. I have to assess how much of the network still exists and see if I can rebuild the broken parts and relocate them somewhere else. If Blanco and Mendoza tracked me, others may have, too. Connie and Christine want to come with me. I think that will be good for them, at least as a transition. They have their own issues to work out. Maybe helping other women with similar problems is one way to go. They certainly understand the problems. They said they don't care where we go at first. After that, I don't know where things will take them."

"You know, I may be able to help you," Frank said. "I mean, just as a friend, no strings, no promises."

"That would be nice," Cheryl said with a smile, "but what I need is money. I've been thinking about a fund-raising plan. It won't be easy."

"Well, let's see what happens," Frank said, with a smile of his own. Then the smile turned to sadness.

"What's troubling you, Frank? I can see it in your eyes, something's wrong." she said.

They sat and just looked at each other across the table. "I lost Kenny's journal. I had it wrapped in plastic and taped to my back when we jumped off the *Celtic Mistress.* But it's gone now, lost in the water. I'm sorry," Frank said. "All those women, lost out there," he said. "I am truly sorry."

"You tried, that's what's important. I'll work harder with the network to try and find them. What about you, Frank? What will you do?" she asked.

"Police work is all I know. I don't want to go back to the department. I *can't* go back to the department. There is just too much bureaucracy, politics and crap like that. I guess I want to help people, too. It's all I ever wanted to do. I just do it in a different way than you. I've been thinking about hanging out my own investigator's shingle," Frank continued. "I have some money, I don't need a lot. If I'm on my own, I can get to pick and choose my cases," he said. "It's a thought."

"You're one of the good guys, Frank. Don't ever lose that quality. Maybe I don't fully understand. Maybe the world needs guys like you who can fight for the little people. I shouldn't be so judgmental. You have to do what feels right for you," Cheryl said.

Frank smiled at her and reached across the table. He took both her hands in his. They continued to stare at each other until they both blushed.

"Thank you," he said.

"I'm the one who needs to say thank you. Without you, I don't know where I'd be right now," she said.

The sub quietly cut through the deep water under the cloak of night into the Atlantic Ocean. Eventually it arrived off Block Island Sound, the small body of water between New York, Connecticut and Rhode Island. As dawn broke, the boat passed into Long Island Sound and up the Thames River in Connecticut with little notice from the world around it. The submarine was guided by pilot boats to the sub pens at the submarine base in Groton. Frank,

Cheryl, and everyone else, except Eddie, were now home in the United States.

Nineteen

After they docked in Connecticut, Frank learned from Aikens about Captain Ruiz's role in bringing the MiGs into the rescue. Aikens told him the mission had to end without the official involvement of the United States. Costa Rica, through Captain Ruiz, called upon Cuba to destroy the *cocaineros'* speedboats. Aikens didn't tell Frank his Washington buddy had ordered him to work with the police captain.

Aikens' plan was to bring the *Celtic Mistress* entourage to Bridgeport, where they would be debriefed by analysts from his Washington team. Once back on U.S. soil, they'd be safe from harm. The Mendoza *cocaineros* would not dare to venture onto U.S. soil to take their revenge, he believed.

Before they disembarked from the submarine for the next leg of their journey to Bridgeport, Captain Ruiz announced he wanted to give a fiesta for the group. He said he'd host the party on the docks of Bridgeport before they all went their separate ways.

"We'll have one final time together," the police captain said, "a happy one."

"Maybe that's a good idea," Frank said. "We've all been through a lot."

The captain smiled. "I have something for you when we arrive," he said quietly to Frank.

"What?" Frank questioned.

"You will see, *mi amigo*, you will see," the captain said with a smile as he left to mingle with the others. Frank liked the Costa Rican cop. Even after he was released in Limon, he decided the guy had been just trying to do his job.

Aikens thought it best that everyone travel to Bridgeport on a U.S. Coast Guard cutter, sailing out of New London down Long Island Sound and into Bridgeport Harbor. A U.S. military ship provided the best security. With Aikens' help, one of the smaller commercial docks was to be cleared out for the captain's fiesta. On short notice, the Costa Rican was able to order up a band and a seafood buffet.

The gang from the *Celtic Mistress*, Aikens and Ruiz disembarked from the Coast Guard cutter onto a dock in Bridgeport. A party was waiting, music was playing, and caterers were preparing a barbecue.

"This is very generous of you, Captain," Frank said.

"You wonder how I can afford this?" he asked.

"Well," Frank said cautiously, "After all, a cop's salary in Costa Rica,"

The police captain laughed. You don't know everything, *senor*," Ruiz said, pointing a longneck beer bottle at his new friend. "*Mi familia*," he said, "we are very wealthy. I am from a long line of coffee growers, part of the aristocracy in my country," he explained. "My police career is a way to help my fellow countrymen. I choose not to sit around and pontificate about problems in my country, as others do, even those in my own family."

Frank looked at him with surprise.

"Costa Rica is filled with people who are either very poor or very rich, and the rich are either people of honor or thieves," the cop said. "Unfortunately, some people of honor can also be lazy. I believe that you need to earn the honor of your countrymen. So I serve in *la policia*. That way I can help the people that need the most help. We are a small nation, *Senor* Reardon, but we are not so small that we don't dream of having homes where our children are safe and we can live in peace. As a police officer, I help give my countrymen protection from their own countrymen who would do them harm."

Frank saw a different man than the police captain he met in Limon. He had originally labeled him a hard-ass. He was wrong about Ruiz, very wrong. This was a man with a heart and a desire to do the right thing. Frank was sorry he had misjudged him.

"So that's where the pictures come in, the ones on the walls of your office," Frank said. "You're a guy with connections."

"My family tree can be traced back to the *conquistadors*. I use my family connections to help the people of my country," the police captain said. "It's not a very complicated concept."

"No, just an honorable one," Frank said with admiration.

The two men smiled at each other. A bond had grown between them. Both cops wanted the same things but sought them out in different ways.

"What are your plans, now that you are home in *los Estados Unidos*?" Ruiz asked Frank. "Do you think you'll ever return to my country? We could use a man like you. Maybe you could join my police force."

Frank shrugged. "That's an interesting offer. But for now, I'll pass. I have a few personal matters to follow up on, things left over from before my retirement," he said.

"Yes, this unresolved matter of your wife's death," he said. "*Senor* Aikens mentioned it to me. You have my sympathies for your loss; I apologize for intruding."

"Is there anything that man doesn't know or stick his nose into?" Frank asked.

The captain said nothing.

"If you go after her killer, don't be emotional," he advised.

Frank looked at him. "It won't be emotional, it'll be personal."

Ruiz nodded. "You must do what you must do, *senor*. I wish you *bueno suerte* in your mission. However you handle these matters, stay focused. "

"*Gracias, senor,*" Frank said. "Most people don't understand."

Ruiz nodded again and said nothing more.

Standing on the pier, they stared out onto the waters of the city harbor, sharing the moment and a beer. Coming in from Long Island Sound past the old lighthouse on the strip of land jutting out into the water was a new fishing boat. It was a pure white, twin-engine vessel capable of serious deep-sea fishing.

The boat moved steadily through the harbor. It drew the envy of every fisherman on the water. As the boat moved past the huge utility plant on the western side of the harbor, Frank made out three strings of flags stretched from the sedan bridge to the bow and stern. The boat was fully outfitted with rods and two fighting chairs on the rear deck.

As it made a turn to dock at the pier alongside the Coast Guard cutter, Frank noticed the flags. The single string to the bow was comprised of American flags. The other two strings to the stern were made up of the Costa Rican flag and the Irish tri-color.

"I hope you like the name," Captain Ruiz said with a smile. "I thought it might please you."

Bending over, Frank read the name *Celtic Tica* stenciled in green and gold script across the bow.

"What's this?" Frank asked.

"She is yours, s*enor*. A gift from a grateful country for your help in ridding us of the cancer of illegal *drogas*," Ruiz said. "I employed a Costa Rica idiom and created the name 'little Celtic.'"

"Yeah, I get the idiom. But a gift from your country, Captain?" Frank said.

"Well, on behalf of my country. My family wishes to make this gift since you lost your beloved *Celtic Mistress*," he said.

"Is this legal?" Frank asked Aikens, who was making his way down the pier with a smile on his face.

"The United States government doesn't interfere in the matter of one person giving another person a gift, Frank. Take the boat," he said with a laugh as music played in the background.

Dutch was on the dock sniffing around the new boat when Frank whistled. He snapped his fingers and waved Dutch on board. "A new home, boy, check it out." The dog leapt aboard and ran around sniffing out every corner of the vessel.

Everyone celebrated their return to the United States well into the night. The crew of the Coast Guard cutter joined the party, as did some of Frank's friends from the police department.

Later, Frank left the party at the dock that christened the new *Celtic Tica*. He felt the need to be alone, to walk the streets of Bridgeport. The old industrial city had given him so much over the years. It also had taken a great toll on him. As a cop, he walked the streets day and night helping people, arresting people, investigating crimes against people. On the flip side, it was in Bridgeport that he lost Susan to a madman who was still free and maybe walking these same streets.

Frank stopped into a bar not far from the docks owned by a retired cop, Bennie Jarvis. Before he left town for Costa Rica, Frank had asked Bennie to store a trunk for him.

"Frankie! It's true, you're home," the retired cop called out when Frank walked into the bar.

"Yeah, I'm back. How's business?"

"Still serving drunks, day in, day out," Bennie said.

Frank leaned over the bar and quietly asked "Do you still have my trunk?

"Right where you left it," Bennie said. "Still locked and in the back room next to my desk."

Frank smiled and strolled into the back room. He spun the dial back and forth on the combination lock, and it snapped open. Inside the trunk were notebooks from old cases, his old badge, some shirts and two .38 caliber revolvers, both of them fully loaded. Frank put one in a holster and clipped it on his belt.

"Feeling better dressed now?" Bennie asked Frank when he came back into the bar.

"Yes, I am," Frank said, smiling.

The two old friends talked about fishing for a while as Frank nursed a beer. He never brought up the Mendoza incident.

Finally, he left the bar and headed up through the back streets leading away from the dock to the city's downtown. He crossed Main Street alongside the New England Bank Tower office building and strolled through McLevy Green toward Runyon's Bar. The tavern was just across the street from McLevy Hall, an old Greek revival-style city building.

Cutting through the vest-pocket park to Runyon's, Frank eyed two men approaching him. The man on his right stayed in the open as the man on his left started to circle around to his rear. Frank slowed and slipped his hand into his coat for the gun strapped on his belt.

"I wouldn't do that, *senor*," the voice of a third man coming out from behind a tree softly declared. "They are faster than you and better positioned," the voice advised.

The other two men in the small park stopped and took up strategic positions covering Frank. Stopping dead in his tracks, Frank chuckled.

It was Mendoza.

"You find this amusing, *senor*?" the drug kingpin asked as he emerged from behind the tree. "Maybe I should give you something to laugh about, *si*?"

"I had my doubts you were dead. You never struck me as the kind of guy to die easy," Frank said.

"*Si, senor*, I pay others to die for me. And I never believed you died on the open water on your fishing boat. So where else could you be? Old strays always come home, isn't that true, *senor*?" Mendoza said with a sneer. "And here we are, in your *ciudad*. Your meddling has cost me a great deal, Reardon. That's why I'm here to handle this *mano-y-mano*," Mendoza said. "It's more honorable, no?"

"You don't have that much honor, Mendoza. Don't hand me a bunch of Latin machismo crap. You are a dishonorable thug, plain and simple. You disgrace your heritage," Frank scolded him. "What are these two monkeys for? You're not telling me they are here to guarantee fair play, are you? Take your best shot," Frank challenged Mendoza.

The drug lord grew visibly angry. He clenched his fists at the insult. Glaring at Frank, he quickly drew a weapon from inside his coat.

Frank slammed his palms on Mendoza's chest at the sight of the gun. The body blow forced Mendoza to reel backward. As the *cocainero* back-stepped, Frank reached for his own gun. He stumbled, too, recoiling from pushing the drug dealer. He caught his heel on a broken sidewalk and fell. He rolled on the ground and rushed to get up, making it to one knee. The few seconds Frank expended in his stumble were more than enough for Mendoza to regain his balance, get a good grip on his gun, and take aim at Frank.

"*Adios, Senor* Reardon! You've caused me enough trouble," Mendoza said angrily, leveling his handgun at Frank.

Frank peered up into the barrel of the weapon and saw Mendoza lifting his head in a laugh. Then the sound of a single rifle shot pierced the night's silence. A bullet ripped into Mendoza's throat and a stream of blood spurted out in an arc from his neck. A second shot rang out in the night and hit Mendoza above the bridge of his nose, right between his eyes.

Between the two shots, Frank was able to draw his own gun. Mendoza hit the pavement in a heap. Frank quickly rolled over on the sidewalk and took aim at the *cocainero's* man closest to him. The burly man was running toward him with a gun drawn. Frank squeezed off two rounds from his snub-nosed revolver and killed the man. He rolled on the ground again, started to stand, and ducked a round fired by the second man. Coming fully up onto one foot, Frank fired another two rounds at his second attacker. Hit in the chest by the bullets, the attacker spun around and flopped onto the grass, dead.

Now kneeling on one knee, Frank surveyed the area around him. Three men lay dead on the pavement and grass. He scanned the area for other attackers. He saw none. A few people outside the bars smoking cigarettes had heard the shots. Some were scattering from the scene and others were approaching, not seeing Frank in the dark, still in a combat shooting position. In the distance there were the sounds of approaching sirens. Someone had called the cops even before Frank's gun barrel cooled.

The police cars rolled up, and cops jumped out of their cars with guns drawn. Frank stood still, held his own weapon in the air and surrendered. Uniformed cops secured the downtown green space and took Frank to a police car. As Frank was placed in the rear seat of a cruiser, his friends from the dock party pushed their way through the crowd, some speaking to police. On the edge of the crowd, he spotted Aikens.

Frank was taken to headquarters for questioning. He refused to speak. Frank wanted to slow things down until he assessed the situation and determined exactly what happened on McLevy Green. He wasn't sure how much of his activities in Central America he wanted known in Bridgeport. A collection of cops shot questions at Frank, Sometimes repeating rapid fire what someone had asked earlier. They had three dead bodies and few answers. The cops had already identified Mendoza through police databases and the Internet as the big fish he was in the drug world. Now he was a shooting victim in their own backyard.

While it appeared clear that Frank had acted in self-defense in killing Mendoza's two henchmen, none of the cops were able to figure out who actually shot Mendoza. Finally, Chief of Police Richard Howell came in and assumed control of the questioning.

"So what do we have here?" the chief asked openly once he was in the room and in charge.

Frank sat in silence.

Don Pruka, Frank's old partner, stood in the corner of the interrogation room. Finally, he suggested they allow Frank to give his statement the next day, after everyone had a chance to get some sleep.

"It might be a way to get a statement without having that fed, Aikens, peering over our shoulders," Pruka suggested. "Reardon just might let something slip."

"Don, I know you and he were partners. He won't give up anything more tomorrow. We work him tonight," Howell said, immediately dismissing the suggestion and returning to the interrogation room.

Back inside, the chief renewed the questioning.

A detective came in and placed a sniper rifle on the table. The weapon, someone explained, was found on the rooftop of a downtown building. The caliber of a bullet from the weapon appeared to be identical to the caliber of the bullets that killed Mendoza. The detective said comparison tests of the bullets from Mendoza's body and those of the weapon found on the rooftop were expected to verify it was the murder weapon. The location where the rifle was found matched, at least preliminarily, the trajectory of the Mendoza kill shots, the detective said.

Frank just listened. While the cop spoke, he strained his eyes to study the stock of the rifle. Finally he saw it. Scratched in the metal butt plate of the weapon was the letter T. It was easily missed or mistaken for an errant blemish in the metal, but Frank was sure of what he saw. It was clearly a T.

"You know, Frank, not many people could have made a shot like that. At first I thought there was a Mendoza guy trying to back shoot you, but that second hit was pretty well clear of you," the cop said with suspicion. "Who could have made that kind of shot?"

Frank remained silent.

"Frank, what happened out there between you and these guys? I want to know," the chief said calmly.

"Am I under arrest?" Frank asked.

The police chief bristled. Frank's do-it-alone style of police work was well known among the department cops. The chief was determined not to let Frank walk out without explaining matters.

"Not yet, Frank. Not yet, and don't make me rethink that status."

Frank said nothing more, nor did he ask for a lawyer.

A uniformed cop came in and whispered in the chief's ear there was someone in the hall waiting to see him. As the door opened and closed, Frank saw it was Aikens.

After a brief inspection of his credentials and more whispering with the chief, Aikens was ushered into the interrogation room. Although a stranger in Bridgeport, Aikens strutted around as if he owned the city.

Turning to his guest, the chief said, "Mr. Aikens, you're being granted some leeway in this investigation because of your position in Washington and your interest in this Mendoza character. While I'm extending you some professional courtesy in this matter, understand something from the start. This is and will remain a local investigation."

Howell was a professional cop. He rose to the rank of lieutenant in New York City, jumped around as an assistant chief in several places, and finally became chief in Bridgeport. "And," he added, "I'd appreciate any light you might be able to shed on these matters. I suspect your presence in town means you know something."

Aikens nodded.

"I must say, however, it does appear this Mendoza guy was shot by someone other than Frank Reardon," the chief conceded.

The Washington intelligence officer understood immediately. "Chief," Aikens said, "it appears to me the situation is clear."

"It is?" the chief shot back, losing his patience. "Why don't you explain it to me? Explain to me why I have three dead bodies in a morgue and some high-powered, mysterious D.C. guy in my police headquarters."

Frank smiled at Aikens.

Aikens sighed and said, "Yes, there are three bodies. You have to agree, however, the three men were shot by two different weapons. Mr. Reardon only shot two men in self-defense because they shot at him. The third man, who we all agree was shot by someone with this rifle you recovered, is the mystery. Ballistics will probably show Mr. Mendoza was shot from a great distance and obviously not by Mr. Reardon."

"But he knows who shot this guy!" the chief roared. "I strongly suspect he and Mendoza had some shared history in Costa Rica."

"Ah, yes, I see your dilemma, chief. However, here's the situation. Mr. Reardon is covered by a federal security blanket for a variety of matters, including some matters of recent times in Central America. Anything he may know is off limits to you. And trust me, since there is evidence demonstrating he didn't shoot Mendoza, you have no chance of getting access from any federal agency to any information pertaining to any alleged history they may have shared in Central America."

"Mr. Aikens," the chief said through clenched teeth, "I want to know why this drug dealer came to my city to shoot this man, and I want to know right now."

Aikens stood silent. Finally, he simply said, "Chief, I am afraid you have just made an inquiry that cannot be answered by anyone in this room. It's just that simple."

The federal agent watched the police chief eye Frank. As the chief drew a breath to speak, Aikens stepped behind Frank.

"He can't tell you. If he answers you he faces a host of federal charges for violating homeland security, chief."

Frank continued to smile in silence.

Twenty

Frank was in police custody all night being grilled. He did not vary from the story that he shot two men in self-defense and didn't know who shot Mendoza. Finally, after he gave a simple statement approved by Aikens, the cops let him go. He admitted knowing Mendoza in Costa Rica, nothing more. As Aikens and Frank left police headquarters on Congress Street early the next morning, both men stopped and took a deep breath of the cool air.

"Well, Mendoza is dead. That has to please you," Frank mused. "Too bad about the dummy computer network you tried to sell him. It looks like that part of your foreign policy plan flopped," Frank said.

"What do you mean?" Aikens asked.

"Your phony network. He's dead, and no one is tapping into it," Frank said.

"Not a problem, it's more viable than ever now. The word will go out Mendoza was killed for it. His competitors will gossip about it for a while. Sooner or later one of them will wonder where it is, what happened to it, and try to find it. In a while, the disc will pop up on the market again and become available," he explained. "We've created market demand for it. We'll offer it for sale again."

"And how many people will be killed as part of this little game you have concocted?" Frank asked.

"I'm going to ignore that question," Aikens said.

The two men were quiet as they stood on the street corner in the morning breeze. "It was him, wasn't it?" Reardon finally asked Aikens. "It was Eddie who shot Mendoza," Frank said on the street corner.

The intelligence chief just looked at him as the sun rose over the city's harbor and said nothing.

"He's alive, isn't he?" Frank pressed.

"The last time I saw him was on a monitor aboard the *Long Island*. He was jumping off your boat just before it was hit by an RPG."

"All that stuff about him being out of the business, the sniper business, true or false? He once told me he was through with sniper work. He was very adamant about it. But we both know it was him last night. I saw the T scrawled on the butt of the rifle the cops found. That's his mark. What made him return to sniper work?"

"You know, Mr. Reardon, I shouldn't even be talking to you anymore."

"He's alive, isn't he?" Frank said, demanding an answer.

"Yes," Aikens said reluctantly. "He's alive. When the Zodiacs from the sub rescued you and the others, one slipped away with him and took him to shore. That's it, you get no more details about his escape," he said. "As long as everyone thought he was dead, including Mendoza, I was able to protect him. If you open your mouth about him, and he gets killed, it's on you. That's the price you have just paid to satisfy your curiosity. I hope you are happy now."

"How'd you get him to work with you again?" Frank pressed.

Aikens stopped and looked up and down the Bridgeport streets outside police headquarters. He saw that they were empty. Dawn was starting to break over the Pequonnock River running through the city's gritty downtown district.

He paused and said, "OK, a long time ago he killed a kid by mistake. It tore him up; that's why he quit. But it was a mistake, a terrible mistake. He was a wreck after that shooting. He never wanted to hold a gun again," Aikens said.

"But you made him, didn't you," Frank said accusingly.

"I explained to him he had a talent, one his government might need sometime. Don't get all teary-eyed with me, Reardon. You've stepped over the line for something you felt was a greater good a few times, too. Didn't you threaten to feed one of Mendoza's men to the sharks? Wasn't that playing God, too?" Aikens asked Frank. "So just lighten up. Mendoza killed kids with complete abandon by selling drugs. I used a simplistic but truthful argument to bring Eddie back into our service. Once I did, and unlike ever before, he only took assignments with a defined purpose, a purpose he could understand," Aikens said.

"You knew Mendoza was still alive. You staked me out as bait here in Bridgeport and had Eddie shoot him. How'd you arrange for all of us to be in McLevy Park? Eddie had to know where we'd be to get the kill shot."

"Research, Aikens said. "Eddie was poised to stay on that roof until you went to Runyon's. We knew it was a joint you patronized."

"How'd you know I'd have a gun?" Frank asked.

"That was sheer luck for us," Aikens said. "We were counting on Eddie getting all three before you were shot."

Frank stood there with his mouth wide open.

"I believed Eddie was that good with a rifle," Aikens said. "It was a risk I took."

"So I was a lamb staked out for the slaughter," Frank said with a laugh. "You guys are something else. Eddie wasn't part of this mess in Central America to babysit me," he said bluntly. "You sent him to take down Mendoza. And when he didn't complete the job in Costa Rica, he came here to Bridgeport. That shot was his assignment, but you would have preferred the shooting took place in another country. Just tell me, where is he now?"

Aikens just stared at him. "I had a job to do, and I did it, plain and simple. Greco's team did find a crashed and burned SUV and a guy in an Armani suit. It was a set-up. Mendoza was hurt, and he dressed one of his dead men in his clothes at the scene. He used his own blood to help stage his death with a guy in the SUV that died. The dead guy's face was severely burned. Mendoza hoped we'd think it was him who died, only the dead guy was an inch shorter than Mendoza. Greco picked up on the height discrepancy, despite the burned face. Greco is very thorough in the field," Aikens said."

Frank laughed. "Christ almighty, Aikens, get a life. How do you live with this much cloak and dagger stuff?"

"You can be a real piece of work, too. Aren't you being a bit high and mighty?" Aikens said. "You know, it was your pal in D.C. that set up the rescue with the submarine and the MiG jets. He called me and brought in Captain Ruiz to arrange things with the Cubans."

"Really?" Frank said calmly.

"Yeah, he didn't give me his name, but I knew the voice. That little jerk I banished to San Jose rifled the phone records and confirmed it was him who called the embassy when the cops first pinched you. Your pal is a pretty big trump card to be carrying around. I did some checking, too. I know why he's good to you. You pulled his kid out of a drug mess."

"That was a long time ago," Frank said.

"Maybe, but he's loyal to you. Don't worry, though. I won't embarrass him," Aikens said.

"Smart on your part," Frank said. "He's a guy with a long memory for good and bad things that happen to him. Get my drift?" Frank asked.

"Yes, I do," Aikens said. "You buried evidence to protect his kid and his reputation. Just like Eddie, you're burdened with a conscience."

"Where is he?" Frank asked again, cutting off the conversation about his Washington connection. "Where is Eddie?"

"Time for us to part company, sir," Aikens said, walking away. He paused and turned back.

"I hear Tyrell Points in Appalachia is a pretty place. Ever hear of it? It's supposed to have good fly fishing, if that sort of thing appeals to you. I'd wait until the spring, however."

Frank stood on the street and watched Aikens turn and walk away. Then he stopped again.

"One more thing, just so you don't think I am a complete amoral slug. I found Kenny's leather journal taped to your back when you were sleeping on the sub. I don't know how many of the women we can find, but we'll do what we can. Tell your lady friend we've already recovered one woman. She's on her way back to the States. We'll relocate her anywhere she wants away from her husband. She will get a new identity and enough money to get a new start in life."

"Thanks," Frank said.

"Too bad your lady friend doesn't have some funding to get that underground network off the ground," Aikens said wryly. "Some of that seed money that Mendoza's people were passing around sounds like it would be enough to get the ball rolling."

"You never know," Frank said. "She just might find an anonymous donor."

Aikens smiled. He suspected Frank had located Patty's drug money in Limon and probably had used Hector to ship it to him. Mendoza's money, the intelligence boss assumed, gave Cheryl almost five hundred thousand dollars to finance a new underground network.

"Good luck with that," Aikens said now. "It would be comforting to believe that somehow bad money might be put to good use."

Meet Author John J. Gilmore

John J. Gilmore writes fiction based on the offbeat people he meets in his travels. He was born and raised in New York City and now lives in Stratford, Connecticut. He spends a great deal of time in Vermont. He spent years as a reporter covering everything from police news to national political campaigns and was an award-winning columnist.

John currently works in law firm marketing and has handled media and crisis communications for lawyers. He has won a number of awards for his short stories, which have been published in *Penworks, Vermont Ink* and *Umbrellastories.com.*

Breinigsville, PA USA
27 December 2010
252107BV00001B/1/P